C0-DKM-871

DISCARD

MAVERICK CANYON

Center Point
Large Print

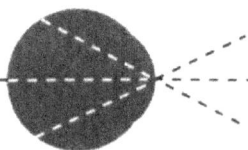

This Large Print Book carries the
Seal of Approval of N.A.V.H.

MAVERICK CANYON

Clem Colt

CENTER POINT LARGE PRINT
THORNDIKE, MAINE

This Center Point Large Print edition
is published in the year 2023 by arrangement with
Golden West Inc.

Copyright © 1944 by Nelson C. Nye.
Copyright © renewed 1971 by Nelson C. Nye.

All rights reserved.

Originally published in the US by Phoenix Press.

The text of this Large Print edition is unabridged.
In other aspects, this book may vary
from the original edition.
Printed in the United States of America
on permanent paper sourced using
environmentally responsible foresting methods.
Set in 16-point Times New Roman type.

ISBN 978-1-63808-699-4 (hardcover)
ISBN 978-1-63808-703-8 (paperback)

The Library of Congress has cataloged this record
under Library of Congress Control Number: 2022951551

Contents

Chapter 1

"LET HIM BE—"

This was Kurt Ruddabaugh's WHEEL HOUSE BAR in Old Town where three men sat eyeing a standing fourth while a gathered, built-up silence choked the smoky back room with menace.

Three men—Phil Haigler, big, rugged, hard with a brash, high-handed arrogance, engineer-representative of Crow-Rondack; Bronc Forney, the irascible Y Bench super, in a slouch hat, checked shirt, boots and Levi's, and with the butt of a double-action Colt boldly showing at a hip; Joe Karvel, with the carelessly assured manner bred of vast experience, and looking a deal more like a surveyor, a construction engineer or the owner of some prosperous dude ranch than the hard-fisted range boss of an operating cow spread. These three. And the standing Buck Fiori, a hired-gun hombre who a scant few moments earlier had come barging in there from the bar with his unwelcome news.

Phil Haigler took a look around and muttered, "Yeah," reluctantly. He left off paring his nails and closed the gold penknife with a snap, stowing it in a pocket of his flower-embroidered vest while a reflective light slowly grew and deepened in his half-closed, watchful eyes.

"Who is the fellow, anyway?" asked Karvel. "Where'd he come from?"

Fiori, with the too loud laugh of a man holding exaggerated ideas of his own importance, said: "He calls himself Rush Rago. He's a long-geared pelican an' claims to be huntin' the mother lode." His curled grin got a little wider as he added: "Where he comes from ain't been mentioned—but a wink's as good as a nod to some of us mules."

Forney, the Y Bench super, said explosively: "The man's got to be put out—put out or—" He left the rest unsaid and matched Fiori's grin with a scowl.

As though he had not spoken, Karvel asked: "Any particular significance, Buck, in that crack about him claimin' to be hunting the mother lode?"

Curly Joe Karvel was foreman of the Y Bench Cattle Company, and, next to Forney, had as much say as anyone in the running of this man's country, but Fiori, a pistol-pusher whom Phil Haigler had bought for eighty a month and found, looked at him with a condescension only a hair's breadth removed from open pity. "This Rago's so blame ignorant he couldn't tell dung from wild honey—an' he puts out t' be huntin' *gold*."

"That settles it!" Forney snapped. "Huntin' gold in copper country! The man's a goddam spy! I say—"

"What you say's of no importance," Haigler cut in coolly. "It's what you figure on doing that'll be of interest to Crow-Rondack. An' the less you do," he said very softly, "the better it'll be for all concerned."

Forney's cheeks showed fire. "You tryin' to dictate Y Bench policy?"

Haigler shook his head. "I'm tryin' to make you see a simple truth. Hang onto your shirt an' think this out for a moment—all of you. This situation's loaded with dynamite. This ain't the time for no tomfoolery. We got to move real slow an' easy or the fat'll be in the fire. This is the one time we can least afford to attract attention; one careless act or word and the whole damned camp will tumble to what we're up to. You don't want to see that happen, do you?"

He paused and looked from Forney's glowering eyes to the cool indifference that sat on Karvel's healthy cheeks. He said: "For once, Bronc, use your head for somethin' besides a hatrack. Look at this reasonably. A stranger shows up prowlin' through the hills with a cock-an'-bull story about prospectin' gold. All right, it looks screwy; I'm willing to grant you that. But there's just a chance that pilgrim's on the level. But whether he is or not, I say let him alone. Let him be till we see what's under his openers."

The ruffled silence resettled, strengthened.

Then Fiori said, regarding them sourly: "I can

tell you what he's got hid under his openers—a goddam gun! I seen him pick off a rattler's head at forty paces. I never even see him throw his rod; just *wham!*—an' the damn snake's head come off like a clap of lightnin'."

Haigler shrugged disinterestedly, but Forney's irascible temper showed in the gleam of his challenging eyes. "You goin' to leave a gun slammin' fool like that loose in these hills to stumble onto things?"

"What'll he find? If you'll sit tight an' keep your mouth shut—"

"It ain't me," Forney snarled, "that'll be lettin' off the blat."

Haigler slowly turned to face him, all expression ironed off his face. Half wheeled that way, he cast a wide and bulky shadow against the wall. And the knuckles of his big fists shone like lumps of ice.

Joe Karvel drawled: "Keep your shirt on, Phil. You know—"

"Keep out of this, Joe," said Forney tightly. "When I want your help I'll ask for it." He looked at Haigler wickedly, his breath a gusty sound. He threw his accusation full in Haigler's teeth with all his headlong rashness. "If there's any leak it'll be no fault of mine, by God—it'll come from your devilin' of that fool girl."

For one of the few times in his life Joe Karvel, a man whose tanned, intelligent face and easy smile proclaimed him a person hard to surprise, felt a keen astonishment. He fully expected an explosion, and his square jaw sagged when a slow smile mellowed the bulldog grip of Haigler's features.

Crow-Rondack's man said easily: "I guess we better go to bed, Bronc, before this wrangling assumes the dimensions of a first-class brawl."

But Forney showed the stubbornness of his rash nature. "We'll go to bed when we get this business settled. 'F you want to horse around with that back-country baggage, I reckon it's your own business so long's you keep your lip buttoned. But what we do about this Rago gent's as much my concern as yours. I say play safe an' rub the ranny out!"

"An'," Phil Haigler remarked very softly, "I say leave him strictly alone."

Bronc Forney glared. "Since when you been runnin' this business?"

"I'm not trying to run it. But neither am I going to stand aside and see you ruin it with your bull-headed blundering." He looked at Forney coldly. "Get this through your head right now. Any time this outfit's up against a question of policy, I'm the one that'll shape it."

"Says you!"

"Says me." Crow-Rondack's man took a cigar from the breast pocket of his coat and bit the end off coolly while he eyed the brick-faced Forney with a bright and narrow stare. "And any time you don't like it you can cut your stick."

"Like that, eh?"

"Just like that."

"By God," said Forney bitterly, "an' to think I was the one rung you in on this." He half reached toward his hip, the light in his straw-colored eyes turning violent.

Haigler laughed at him. "Go ahead if you think you can cut it. Be on a par with the rest of your hare-brained notions."

For a long moment the Y Bench super held his strained, belligerent pose, then wheeled with a strangled curse and poured himself a stiff drink from the bottle on the table.

Karvel rose then, saying: "Reckon I'll turn in," and started for the door.

"Good idea if we all turned in," Haigler nodded.

"An' you're goin' to let that imitation prospector keep right on a-prospectin'?" demanded Fiori, scowling.

"Until I say otherwise—yes," Haigler said, and smiled at Forney's back.

Chapter 2
A VOICE FROM THE CLIFF

It was getting on toward the shank of the evening, and Rush Rago, who'd spent most of that day as well as all the three preceding ones prowling through the tumbled chaos of these Burro Mountains, told himself for the hundredth time that the life of a canary-following coffee-cooler was no bed of roses.

He'd been tramping upthrust hills and rocky gulches since dawn and was so dog-tired his knees threatened to buckle at every boot-hurting step he took. If the burros hadn't been so confounded little he'd have ridden one of them instead of alternately carrying and bitterly heaving away sundry portions of their bulging packs.

He scowled at the mile-long shadows being thrown by a dying sun and snorted. Another day gone to hell, and not a sale or smidgin of ore to show for all these blistering miles. He sure would like to bet both hands wrapped round the gizzard of that squirt who'd claimed there was gold in these damn hills!

He was tall and gaunt, a brockle-haired man with a high tough face and freckled nose. He had a rider's stiff-hipped grace, a wide mouth and guileless eyes that could upon occasion induce extreme uneasiness in the recipient of their attention. His clothes, patched and faded, were shrunk by many a washing; but there were silver gut hooks on his boots, and the big forty-five slung low on his thigh showed a butt both smooth and shiny.

He'd had a good job back in Texas punching other people's cattle—had been due, in fact, for the top screw's bunk and probably would have got it if that bonanza-spouting burro-chaser hadn't blown into the Four Aces bar that night while he'd been liquidating a pay check. It made him boil every time he recalled that fellow's whoppers. Why, for two cents—

And right there was where the slug from a high-powered rifle scattered his reflections like hay before a Kansas twister. It struck with a jarring force that knocked rock splinters screaming from an outcropping just beyond his shoulder. The burros halted and snorted, then went off like a flight of locusts; but Rush Rago wasn't noticing—he was digging himself into cover with the echoes of that shot gyrating loudly in his ears.

It would be just his luck to be caught like this unheeled. His rifle was on one of the burros, but it might as well have been in China for all the good it was likely to do him now.

There was no doubt in his mind where that

14

shot had come from. There was a little cave tucked away up there in one of those red-rock cliffs; close to the rim it was, and well above the tumbled chunks that had rotted from its face and fallen like a giant's blocks to well nigh choke the sandy bottom of this once-a-year river's bed.

Of course, that hole up there might not be a cave, but it sure looked like one from here; looked like those cliff-dweller ruins he had seen one time up at Puye.

He leaned out to get a better look, and something jerked the floppy brim of his disreputable old black Stet hat. He ducked back with a curse, but not without seeing the telltale puff of smoke that curled from the black hole's mouth.

He wished to heaven he had that rifle. A six-gun wasn't much use against a .30-.30—particularly at this distance and angle. He might as well have a pop-gun!

The shadows lengthened. A dove whistled in the blue salt cedar off to the right. Rush stayed where he was and ground his teeth and thought of a number of things he'd take pleasure in doing to a guy who'd pop another without due warning. But he kept down back of his rock. When it came to this kind of business, he had the patience of an Indian.

Five minutes dragged the way of all minutes in this life. Another ten cruised slowly by. Rush wondered if the fellow had slid out on him. It would be just like that kind of coyote to fire and run. He grimaced at the notion and fingered the butt of his six-gun longingly. This unwarranted attack had whetted up his temper to a fine point. All the piled-up frustration of this crazy hunt was culminating in the wish to get his gun's sights lined on a certain chuckawalla who holed up and blasted away at chance wayfarers like a rattleweed-smoking Hopi.

But he knew better than to pit his pistol against that long-range .30-.30.

The shadows thickened, curdled; slowly turned from blue to purple. Dusk hunkered down upon the country, and still no further sign came from the unknown marksman in the cliff. Rago's Job-like patience began to wear a little thin.

He poked his hat up on a stick, and nothing happened.

Feeling a bit more confident, he edged a look around his rock. The silence remained unbroken save for the increasing activity of scratching insects making ready for a bedtime chorus.

Rush guessed that whoppy-jawed highbinder must have sure enough pulled his freight, and with a disgusted oath got grumbling to his feet. But the way he got back down behind the rock again shamed lightning by comparison. There was a new rent in his shirt, and the hemming cliffs were full of clamor. Rush's soul was full of fury as he poked a finger through the hole.

It made him boil to be cooped up this way like a chicken waiting to get its neck wrung.

Gritting the choicest of his private cusswords, he squinted round about to see if there was any other cover he could get to that would give him greater vantage.

But there wasn't. The nearest covert other than his own was over thirty feet away—a pasear too far to contemplate while that lead-throwing hydrophobia skunk sat waiting for a further chance to demonstrate his shooting talents.

Rush lifted up his voice and bellowed: "What the hell's the big idear?"

But the only answer vouchsafed him was the echo of his own words banging off the cliffs.

Then he got an inspiration. Maybe if he pretended that he was ready to back-trail himself, that bird would keep his damned lead in his gun and let him go.

He began a cautious backward crawling. Ten tedious feet of this brought him to a point where he could see over his sheltering rock and view the hideout of the bushwhacker. Sure now the fellow could see him—even considering the poorness of the light—Rush got to his feet and put both hands above his head as token of his peaceful intentions.

It was gall and wormwood to his soul to confess it, but he had no craving for a drygulch grave. He shouted: "Save your lead—I'm headin' back."

It got no more answer than had his former attempt at parley.

He said: "Mind if I hunt my critters first? I got a lot of stuff on them I wouldn't like to lose."

He waited several seething seconds, then snarled: "Well, damn you—say somethin'! *Can I?*"

"No!"

Rush stared while his heart did a couple of flip-flops.

That ornery bushwhacker was a girl!

Chapter 3
RUSH MAKES TRACKS

"Well, I'll be damned," Rush said.

And before he could work up further indignation the cool, calm tones of the girl assured him: "You most certainly will less'n you turn yo'self around an' head on back wheah you came f'om. An' you better turn right pronto or I'm a-goin' to blow a window through yo' hatrack."

"You an' who else?" Rush scoffed.

"Jest me alone, confound you! Guess you reckoned I wouldn't know you in that get-up. You get on outa here. Get quick!"

Rush shoved back his floppy headgear to scratch puzzled fingers through his brockle hair. There was a queer light in his squinted eyes as he craned his neck in an effort to catch a glimpse of the face behind that menacing, outthrust rifle. But he craned in vain; the girl kept herself out of sight. And while he stood there looking, "My finger's fixin' to get a heap itchy," she warned. "You better be on your way."

Rush looked down at his boots and scowled. Then he turned his gaze on the cliff again. "You got me all wrong, lady. Look—I don't know you from Adam's off ox, an' it's a lead-pipe cinch you don't know me—"

"I know you all I aim to! You're a belly-crawlin' skunk, an' if you don't fetch yo'self out of my sight in one sand-scorchin' hurry, I'm a-goin' to shoot. You want to find a coroner sittin' on you?"

"Well, no-o," Rush said. "But you got me all wrong, ma'am. I'm a stranger round these parts. I'm jest out of Texas. Heard you had a big strike up here an' quit my job to sell picks an' dynamite an' stuff to—"

"So that's your line, is it? A strike, eh? What kind of strike?"

"Gold—"

"Who said so?"

"Some damn ol' desert rat I was buyin' drinks for down to Double Axe the other night. He said—"

"What was his name?"

"Well," Rush said dubiously, "he *claimed* his name was Stevens."

"That old liar!" The girl stepped into view on a little ledge that led down toward the trail, but she held her rifle ready, Rago noticed. "You must be pretty green to follow ary tip that old fool give out. Come over here where I can get a look at you. Here—wait! Throw down that hawgleg first. If you're packin' a knife, throw that down, too. And, mind you now—no monkey business."

Rush laid his pistol in plain sight on the rock and started toward her. He'd hardly progressed a scant six paces when she spoke again.

20

"Remember, mister, I ain't foolin'. First stunt'll be your last. Come slow now an' keep your hands up over yo' ears."

Rush had covered about ten feet when she motioned him to stop. The expression on her countenance as she stood there looking him over was hardly complimentary, but very probably this was influenced by Rago's own rude stare. He was gaping at her astounded.

And with some cause.

The harshness of her tones and easy handling of that rifle had led him to expect some rough, tobacco-chewing, coarse back-country Amazon. Her actual contrast to this preconceived opinion took his breath away.

Young she was, firm-breasted, and clad in faded rags several shades at least more disreputable than Rago's own; they appeared to be the cast-off things discarded by some range tramp. But it was not at her clothes that Rush was looking; it was at the girl herself. A beautiful pagan—a modern personification of Diana; every lithe and rippling curve of her heralded scorn of some convention. And there was an edge of scorn in the caustic way she eyed him.

She said abruptly: "You're not the particular polecat I been lookin' for. But you're a polecat, though, all right or you wouldn't be snoopin' round yere. Jest what are you huntin' for, pilgrim?"

Her stormy beauty captivated Rago. Already he'd forgotten those dire, un-Christian things he'd planned to do to this damn bushwhacker should the tables ever be turned to his advantage. He could think of nothing now but her bewitching loveliness—and she *was* lovely. Like a bar of treasured melody from some half-remembered anthem. Like a desert sunrise—like Texas in the spring. Not even this scant light could hide the flaming red of her unruly hair, the clean white flash of cared-for teeth. Nor could these hand-me-downs that garbed her hide away that slender body's fresh young charm. She was like a wild rose blooming in the sand-locked fastness of those craggy hills.

"Talk up, you! What you doin' here?"

"Uh—er—what?" Rush stammered, looking foolish. "Could you ride that trail again, ma'am? Reckon I was kinda thinkin'—"

"Yeah! I know what you was thinkin'! Same as the rest of these gosh-blame varmints!" she said resentfully, while a sullen flush spread across her piquant features. "Now you leave off. Quit oglin' me an' answer what I asked you."

"Er—ask again, ma'am, will you?"

She scowled in displeasure and hitched her rifle higher. "I wanta know what you're a-doin' round yere—an' don't bother thinkin' up no lies."

Rush sighed. It looked like she was going to

be hard to satisfy. He'd already told the truth, but she wouldn't believe him. He said as much, adding: "If I had them dash-lammed burros here I could prove what I been telling you. I come out here like I said in hopes of sellin' picks an' dynamite an' stuff to the birds that come here gold-huntin' on the news of that big strike."

"An' I tell you there ain't been no strike!"

Rush shrugged. "I can't help that, ma'am. I was told there was."

"By that fool sagebrusher, Stevens? Hell! no one in this locality would believe that so-an'-so on a stack of Bibles six mules high! He was always tellin' whoppers. He got so gosh-blamed bad was why Paw had to fire him—"

"He worked for you?" Rush asked.

"He worked fer Paw. Did odd jobs an' things around the place—what time I wasn't doin' 'em for him. Shiftless, no-account ol' liar; that's what he was. An' when he got to takin' up with that snake's belly of a Haigler, an' tellin' him all that stuff about—"

She broke off suddenly and looked at him suspiciously, a quick fear in her wide glance, her rifle gripped more grimly. "What you mean askin' me all them questions, stranger? You ain't tryin' to pump me, are you?"

"There you go," Rush growled. "All I asked was did that ol' coot work for you. If I'd been tryin' to pump you—"

" 'F I thought you was," she said, her eyes narrowed fiercely, "I'd blast yo' mortal tintype! Quit grinnin' at me, dang you! I make out to be plumb serious. Start hoofin', mister, before I do you a hurt. G'on; turn roun' an' start unravelin' tracks."

"I thought this was a hospitable country—"

"You'll find out diff'rent if you don't hightail it pronto. Beat it! Roll yo' hocks!"

"Shucks, I ain't in no hurry, ma'am." He affected not to notice the warning glint of her too bright eyes. "You can't object to me huntin' my burros. All I got in this cold world is on them critters—"

"You'll have less in the *next* an' find it considerable hotter 'f you don't pull yo' freight this instant."

She said it coldly, without compromise, but Rush grinned at her. She was squinting down the barrel of her Sharps just like the heroine of one of those traveling melodramas; she looked downright grim and earnest, too. But Rush had been around. He knew she wouldn't really shoot him; it was all just front, designed to impress the ignorant.

He widened his impudent, twisted grin in an appreciative chuckle. "Shucks, ma'am. You oughta put that talent on a stage—"

He got that far. The bark of her rifle cut off the rest. The last thing he remembered he was reeling

24

around like a weed-drunk squaw, and there was a roaring in his ears and a tightness in his chest, and the ground was rushing up at him with the speed of the Denver Special.

Chapter 4

CHALLENGE

Since discovery of copper in the hills, the Burro country seemed to have taken a grand new lease on life. Tyrone had blossomed from a backlands cow town to a thriving municipality of some six thousand souls. Most of these were Mexican, brought in from across the Border; but if one could believe the padre in the little frame chapel up the gulch, the Good Shepherd took no heed of nationality when gathering sheep for the fold. The Company, however, with true Christian foresight, quartered most of these laborers in Old Town, away from the public sight, in the tarpaper shacks and soap-box shanties lined with cloth to keep the winds out and with stone-weighted bits of corrugated tin for roofs to shed the summer rains. The part of Tyrone that visitors saw was the new part: the fine new plaza boasting New Mexico's largest department store, the Spanish-architecture tile-lined depot with its stone-flagged, arcaded promenade, swank office building, its two-storied Company headquarters building, up-to-the-minute library, Western Union, meat market and hat-maker's shop. The post office, too, was on this plaza, designed in keeping with the rest, and just a stone's throw from the depot, with a tobacconist and newsdealer's shop between. And the ridges and hilltops roundabout were garnished with gay, pastel-tinted adobes and the fine roomy houses of stucco with screened-in porches where the higher-up officials could sleep if the nights got a little warm. And each ravine, gulch and arroyo had its own double row of stucco boxes to house the families of the middle income bracket.

There was a little park in the plaza's center with foliaged trees and flag-stoned walks and a concrete floor for open-air dancing; and two big floodlights on tall masts so the boys could see to keep their brogans off the ladies' slippers. This, at least, was what Durango, the reticent town marshal, said they were there for. But Kurt Ruddabaugh, owner of the Wheel House Bar in Old Town, had once remarked he guessed the floods had been put there to light Company officials in a crown of glory when they got up to make their frequent speeches—in front of visiting delegations—on the freight-carload of money the Company had spent to see that their help was comfortable and insure them every advantage of "modern life."

Kurt Ruddabaugh was not a Company favorite. He was, in fact, a thorn in the Company's trousers and was only allowed to continue on their land because of his admitted influence with certain of their more valued Mexican labor. A non-conformist and free-thinker was this owner of Old Town's tavern; an imposing figure in his starched white suit of linen. His hair, too, held a starched look; brown it was and bushy, streaked with gray like hoar frost and erect as the tuft between a lynx's ears. There were some who thought him lynxlike in other ways, but it had never been proved conclusively.

Crippled by a bad horse in his younger days, according to rumor, he spent the bulk of his time in a wheel chair with his Mexican patronage and seemed to have plenty of food for thought. Yet when it suited his book he could be as hearty as the next, a hail fellow well met of the first water. He often was with Durango, and once had been with the Y Bench super, Forney. But lately a rift had widened between them, laid by Kurt to ambition without mentioning whose it was. Forney, he said, trailed bets with a different crowd; and he probably knew, for he kept a close pulse on the public temper and was aware of most things that went on. Caught in the right mood, Durango had found him useful.

It was eleven-fifteen of a cool, dark night when the marshal dropped in for his liquor. He stood by the door for a moment, surly and dark, unapproachable. With a sloe-eyed glance that missed nothing he crossed with a nod to Kurt Ruddabaugh, and wheeled Kurt's chair to a corner where the three or four Latins who stood at the bar could not stretch their ears to much vantage. Then he hauled up a chair, and Ruddabaugh ordered the drinks.

"You been thinkin' too much, Durango."

Scowling, the marshal nodded. He had a saddle-whipped leanness and the quick, quiet step of a cat. Thick cartridge belts girded his hips and supported twin Colts in slashed holsters. He had a thin nervous chest and a pockmarked face the color of parboiled leather.

"Bad complex," Ruddabaugh smiled. "Man in your job better do what the Company tells him an' let well enough alone."

"There's things," Durango grunted, "goin' on in this place I ought to know about."

"In the Wheel House?"

The marshal stared at him strangely. "No," he said. "In town."

Kurt grinned in his big slow way. "You losin' your touch with the Company?"

Staring down into his glass, Durango snorted. He said across its rim: "My trouble's with this new sport—Haigler."

Ruddabaugh shook his head. "This is Burro Mountain Copper's town. Haigler's a Crow-Rondack man. Makes him pretty small potatoes."

"Does it? How well do you know him, Kurt?"

"Don't know him at all. He drops around for a drink occasional-like. I don't reckon we've exchanged a dozen words."

"Quit hedgin'," Durango grunted. "I've savvied you quite a spell, Kurt. You size a man quick's you clap your lamps on him."

Ruddabaugh said softly: "What are you getting at?"

Durango stirred. A sway of motion ran along his bony shoulders, disturbing the set of his black silk shirt, causing the long smooth muscles beneath it to ripple lithely like the hide of a turning cat. The stubbornness that was in him showed in the set of his jaw-line, in the gleam of his narrowed eyes and in the way his spatulate fingers suddenly tightened round his glass.

He said darkly: "Him an' Forney an' that Karvel article has been gettin' downright chummy. It don't look right. Them birds got no more in common than a bean, a pea an' a onion. What are they teamin' up about? It ain't natural—you know the way Bronc Forney is."

"Well, Haigler's pretty smooth—"

"Sure he is! That's what I'm gettin' at. So god-dam smooth slick wouldn't melt in his mouth! There's somethin' back of them two hookin' up. A wolf don't hunt with no leopard." He eyed the tavern boss morosely. "Tell you another thing: Forney's actin' edgy as hell. Half hour ago I was standin' in that alley by the bank when him an' Karvel come along with their heads together. I says: 'Hi, Bronc,' like that, an' the damn fool whirled like he was goin' to lead me."

He sat there brooding, swirling the untouched whiskey in his glass. He looked at Ruddabaugh suddenly. "Figured mebbe you might know somethin'."

In the wheel chair Ruddabaugh sat relaxed, his regard upon the ceiling. His hands lay idle on the blanket folded across his knees. Pale hands they were, without calluses—without dirt beneath their shiny nails. He brought his gaze down to them after a moment; gave them a frowning scrutiny. He said at last: "Tough team, Joe. Don't believe I'd prod 'em was I you." He pursed his lips, for a second looking directly at the marshal. "Man who kicks an ant-hill is a fool."

Durango snorted. "I didn't ask you for philosophy—I asked for information." His eyes probed the inn-keeper roughly. "They been usin' this place for a hangout."

"Have they?" Ruddabaugh's glance was bland. "Seems like there's still a few things I wasn't aware of. I knew they'd met here once or twice, sort of casual-like, but—Well, why shove your neck out? The world's a good place if you'll have it that way. You know Bronc Forney, Joe. Better let sleepin' dogs lie—"

"Sure," Durango said. "Leave 'em lie—an' get bit quick's your back's turned." He looked at Ruddabaugh carefully. "Takin' a cut from that bunch, are you?"

Ruddabaugh's chest showed a deepened breathing, but no change marred the genial set of his enigmatic features. Nor did he bother answering. He let the silence go on piling up until Durango growled: "By God, look here, Kurt. We been friends some spell. But you can't run with the hares an' hunt with the hounds. Who you back of, anyway?"

Ruddabaugh's voice was just above a whisper. "You know the answer to that, Joe."

"I don't know anything," Durango snapped. "But I'm gettin' damn suspicious!"

He jerked up out of his chair and whirled to stand over Ruddabaugh grimly. "Look—you can play the Company's tune or you can do your fiddlin' elsewhere."

He flung the tavern man a long, hard look and turned on his heel and left.

The girl stood there unmoving for moments after Rago fell, the rifle hanging forgotten in her hands, a startled light breaking through the wide blue eyes with which she watched that huddled shape. Slowly was borne in upon her consciousness the magnitude of what she'd done; and suddenly she was cowering back, trembling in every limb, incapable of coherent speech or action, conscious only of the blackest horror she had faced in nineteen years.

A nausea crept upon her. Regret, recrimination,

loathing—every instinct in her cried out against the wild impetuosity of her act. She had shot this man! Goaded by his taunting grin, in a moment of flaring anger she had shot this burro-herding stranger. Suppose she'd killed him!

With the breath hung up in her throat she stared, alert eyes seeking out some movement, some faint sign of life.

But there was none. Neither the flicker of an eyelid nor the shallowest breath betrayed that there was life still in him. One arm was doubled under him; the other lay across his breast, obscuring the wound she had inflicted, hiding its blood from her.

The complexity of her emotions carried her forward three or four halting steps. A sudden thought clutched at her, and fear came swiftly on its heels. The law! The law would call this MURDER!

She stared round her wildly with shaking knees. What if they should trap her here? With him! And with this gun!

Her cheeks were deathly white. There was no color in her lips. She eyed the rifle in her hands as though it were a snake and flung it from her and scrubbed her hands upon her clothes as though contact with the weapon had left its brand on her.

That shot! Suppose someone had heard it— were coming, even now, to investigate its source?

Her frightened eyes stabbed the shadows. She must hide—must get away from here!

She willed to leave but could not move. Terror and the complexity of all those other crowding emotions held her rooted. She kept seeing the stranger's eyes as they'd been when she'd shot him—wide with wonder, for a second darkening to scorn, and then as he pitched forward holding some queer admiration.

She could not get them out of mind.

If only the power were given her to undo this terrible wrong. If only she could bring him back! If only she could see him well and, once again, standing as he had been standing, grinning at her impudently.

But wait! She could not leave without making sure that he was dead; without having first convinced herself all chance were lost to save him.

Reluctantly, against her will, she crept slowly forward to sink down by his side. Helpless, horror- and conscience-stricken, she crouched there by him, fear forgotten; filled with pity that a man as young as this should die, shocked and penitent that his death should be at her hands.

A low, strange sound, an alien rasp in all that vast land's stillness, made her shrink her cowering in the shadow of the rock. With the roughness of the boulder's surface pressing her back, she darted dread-filled glances through the swirling gloom while her throat felt parched, she almost strangled, and her pulses jumped to tumult.

Had that been a step or groan?

Her ears hurt with the intensity of her listening, but all she caught was the loud, chaotic pounding of her heart.

Then it came again, and she stared at the sprawled shape wildly. The sound had been a groan. She could not doubt it longer; the stranger lived!

Yes—look there! His arm had moved!

While she watched incredulously, weak and shaking in an excess of relief, she saw him slowly turn, roll over and come with infinite torture to a knee. In his delirium he tried to rise, to get upon his feet. But vainly; already he was sinking back. His legs would not support him. But for the hand clawed into the rock he would have crumpled.

In the half-light they faced each other. She could see how the high tough face with its freckled nose was clammy with sweat and lines of pain. He was ghastly in the gloom; like a ghost, new-risen from the dead. His deep-set eyes looked red-rimmed, sunken; they glowed with a wild, strange light as they searched her face.

"You—you shot me, damn it!" he gasped.

She could not speak. All the words she would have said choked in her throat. There was a cruel tightness across her chest; she scarcely breathed. Only her eyes were alive; they were wide and startled and frightened as she watched him sway there, watched the fight he made to keep from falling, watched his chin sink lower and lower till it stopped against his breast.

She wanted to say something to him—to tell him she was sorry; that she hadn't meant to shoot him; that she'd been driven to it by his grin and by that perverse streak that was in her nature, by that spunky brashness that had been the cause of all her troubles as far back as memory went. But she could not speak; her tongue was parched, unwieldy. She could only stare while a lump rose in her throat and his head sank lower and lower.

Then he was muttering something, husky-voiced, as though each word would be his last. "Do somethin'—damn you—do somethin'! D'you wanta see me die here? Stuff the hole with rags— tie somethin' round me—"

His voice trailed off like a weary child's; and like a child's his hand slipped from the rock and he was sagging forward—was lying there with his hat half off, with his sandy curls against the tawny earth.

Chapter 5

ORDERS FROM A PETTICOAT

The first thing Rago realized when consciousness returned was that he was lying in a bunk beneath a green Chimayo blanket. He lay there a long time with his eyes closed, thinking it over. The fact was strange and held out many possibilities, for he had never owned a green Chimayo and he could not, for the life of him, recall getting into a bunk. Unless he had things terribly snarled he should be right now on the track of gold and gold-hunters—leastways, he remembered leaving Texas with that intention. He could not recall having cancelled it; in a hazy kind of way he seemed to recollect, in fact, having followed burros' rumps for miles and miles and miles. Up hill and down he'd followed those jovial, prank-playing critters; day after day from dawn to dusk he'd plowed through scorching sand and waves of shimmering heat in the wake of those same tail-swinging critters—or had he dreamed all those miles of toil and travail?

He opened burning eyes again for an inventory of his surroundings. He was in a cabin, all right, but it was not the bunkhouse of the 4CJ ten miles out of Double Axe. This was a wide, low room with a rough rock ceiling that had more the look of a cavern than of anything fashioned by a mason's hands.

Damn queer, he thought, observing the two coal-oil lamps bracketed to the far board wall. Then he realized something queerer. By the lamps' mellow light he saw that the wall was made of boxes—wood salvaged from canned crates, giant powder cases and a miscellany of packing boxes. Crazy fool stuff to build a house of, he thought irritably.

He wished that pain in his side would go away; maybe then his head would clear and the facts of his predicament emerge as they truly were. He couldn't remember hurting himself. But that pain was downright urgent. Seemed like a fellow ought to recollect easily how he'd got a bump like that.

His head didn't feel so good, either; he wondered if he'd somehow bumped that, too. And a funny kind of spots of light kept reeling up and down before his eyes. They sort of brought to mind the day he'd taken that swig of forty-rod the new parson had been passing out that time the crusade had come to Double Axe.

Better sleep it off, he guessed, and was about to close his eyes when he became aware that he was not alone in the place; that someone else was there and moving round just outside his range of vision. He started to twist over on his side and found himself unable. It was astounding! Why, he felt as weak as that damn tea with milk the English earl had served him at Banner.

It kind of frightened him to think of being so helpless. What the hell had happened to him? Had somebody beat him up? It was as if he'd been through a barroom brawl, but he couldn't recall the details. That was half the trouble; he couldn't recall a thing.

By grab, it was time he was getting out of this!

Summoning all his will power, he tried to rise to a sitting posture and in the effort of it fainted.

Much later he seemed to hear the drone of far-off voices. One was gruff, abrupt and questioning; the other must have been an angel's. But he was too tired to trouble about finding out. Anyway, the voices were all tangled up with the blood-curdling cries of that band of Apaches who were hunting him; some inner prompting warned him not to open his eyes lest the redskins see him and put him to the stake.

He thought one time a rattlesnake had bit him and he was in Utah someplace and the Mormons were trying to cure him by the laying on of hands. Someone certainly had put a hand on his forehead; it was a nice hand, too. Firm and soft and cool as frost-bitten moss of an early morning. Then someone—it sounded like that angel he'd heard arguing with Old Nick—was saying quietly: "Open your mouth now. Wider. You'll like this and it'll do you a heap of good. That's right. Here—take the rest of it." And something hot and burny was gurgling down his throat like a mountain cataract. But it did him good. It seemed to scare those Apaches off; he could hear the muffled drumming of their wild paint ponies as they thundered up the draw.

When Rago opened his eyes again it was with a sense of change. He was still in the lumpy bunk—still in the unfamiliar box-wood cabin. But there was a difference. The lamps were out and the light of day was warm in the room and he felt better. The pain in his side was not so sharp and his head was a little clearer and the red spots had quit jumping before his eyes.

He felt hungry.

But he didn't try to move just yet. Memory of what had happened the last time he had tried that was still too vivid. And he'd got his fill of Indians.

Lying quite still, he let his glance play round. Damn curious place, this cabin. Lumber must have been scarce that they'd built a shack of packing cases. In a crude way, though, the place looked comfortable; looked almost homey even. There was a kind of tow-sack curtain at the window picked out with a border of blue gentians embroidered in scarlet yarn. He guessed they were blue gentians; they kind of had that shape.

A soapbox cupboard by this window was filled with tinned stuff, and off there in the corner was a .30-.30 rifle that looked cared for and efficient, and an old Greener was hung from a pair of antlers above a closed door.

He became aware that a smell of cookery was in the air, the tempting odor of frying meat pleasantly mingled with the smell of burning sage. Evidently he wasn't by himself here; breakfasts didn't cook themselves that he had ever heard of. He wondered if the fellow was in the room now, if he'd know him—if it was one of the boys from the 4CJ.

Very slowly, very carefully, so as not to bring back the staggers, he turned his head a little. Yes, there was the fellow, now. He was bent above the stove with a long bone-handled fork. The back inside that patched gray flannel shirt and dusty vest was narrow as a boy's; a lithe and somehow graceful sort of back. And the hand with the fork was long and slender, well-tanned by desert suns.

Rago's eyes drifted up to the head and he swore with sudden astonishment. It was not a man bent above the stove—it was a girl!

She must have heard him, low though his grunt had been. For she whipped around.

Rago's eyes snapped wider and his heart set up an increased thumping.

Grab, but she was pretty! Young—slender as a willow pole. A tousled mane of flaming hair topped features of the sort you saw in Sunday papers; proud they were and spirited. Her eyes had the blue of mountain pools at twilight. They were regarding him gravely, alive with wonder, with speculation, with a little anxiety too, he thought.

Somewhat taken at a loss for words by this pleasing apparition, Rago began: "Nice mornin' for this—"

But she cut him off with a quick, alarmed gesture. "Shh!" She put a finger to a pair of lips the color of ripe red cherries. "Better save that tongue-waggin', stranger, till you're stronger. I expect you're on the mend now, but—" She let the rest trail off to ask abruptly: "You feelin' hungry?"

He nodded. "I could eat a cow—hoofs, hide an' horns." He lay there silent for a while, content to watch her, content to listen to her voice. Soft it was, full and throaty like a thrush's—like the purl of hidden waters.

She said: "I'll fix some broth—"

"Broth?" He screwed his face up. "Did you say *broth,* ma'am? How come? What's the matter with givin' me some of that steak you're fryin'?"

"How about lettin' me take care of the grub while you keep a hobble on your jaw? You're supposed to keep still an' take things easy. By Friday, mebbe, if you're strong enough—"

"Strong enough! Say—what's the matter with me, anyhow? I been eatin' meat all my life an'—"

"You ain't eatin' any now," she said, and turned back to her cooking.

Chapter 6

Y BENCH MAKING MEDICINE

In the 1880's an outfit frequently might be described as "great" if it ran anywhere in the neighborhood of a hundred thousand cattle. Such hit-or-miss way of tendering tribute did not obtain when the Burro Mountain Copper crowd took over the Tyrone country; in that day, when Europe's big crowned heads were hunting ways to slice each other's throats, Burro Mountain's yardstick for greatness was concerned directly with the political, economic and moral aspects of a man. At such a time, and under these conditions, were Cowles Proctor and his Y Bench Cattle Company accorded the coveted courtesy.

His ranch headquarters, twenty-odd miles from the little town of Hatchita, was noted for the tales of its hospitality; indeed, yarns of the happenings at this magnificent hacienda were only surpassed by the quixotic quality of the unadorned facts. This place—*La Paloma*—was the home of grandeur; only the handsomest caballeros, the loveliest of ladies, were ever glimpsed within its confines. Proctor had an eye for beauty and, though he entertained on a large scale, picked his guests with care. His leather-bound visitors' book read like a roll of national celebrities, so many of the country's famous personalities were listed there—the foremost musicians, authors, painters, sculptors and playwrights; even a few metropolitan singers had scrawled their names there, and at least one representative of foreign royalty. Not even the Dons of Old Mexico could boast of gayer, more colorful fiestas than those thrown under the old man's patronage. The Y Bench brand rode the flanks of upwards of three hundred thousand cattle, and the ranch itself was one of the largest in the whole southwest; only the King kingdom in Texas came anywhere near approaching it for size.

Cowles Proctor himself was a man who looked stamped out of sun-cured leather, and was dressed that way as well. A man of seventy, he was straight as an arrow, carried himself with an air, comported himself with dignity and was alert as a bright new pin. In a game of wits he seldom came out the loser, and his memory was a thing that might well shame elephants' by comparison.

He had started life in the hard board bed of a Red River cart, and often liked to tell of it to some of those on whom his largesse was showered. Mostly, though, he liked to listen to other folks' talk, and often sat from dusk to daylight engrossed in the narratives of visitors from far-off places. But he was at the peak of delight when arguing with some person the intricacies of foreign diplomacy, national questions of the hour, domestic relations, or things pertaining to cattle and horses.

There was six hundred thousand dollars' worth of fence around the Y Bench acres; there were over three hundred wells upon the property, many of them artesian, others pumped by windmills and a few by gasoline. Five crews of men were kept at work with special trucks, spending all their time in the service of these waterholes. The cost of the horses, saddles, gear, automobiles, guns and buildings on the place would have run to millions. A couple of millions at least had been spent on land-clearing machinery and roads. No man could estimate Cowles Proctor's worth or even guess the true value of the Y Bench.

Like his forerunners and many of his contemporaries, Proctor had started out with longhorns brought from Texas. More shrewd than most, he had early seen the advisability of putting less grass in horns and more in what the market paid for. Gradually through the years he had graded up his herds, replacing the wild, gaunt Texas stock with meatier breeds from Europe and with a distinct new breed of his own until Y Bench beef found the top of the market everywhere.

His hands, for the most part, were Mexican; vaqueros than whom there were no finer—men who made careers of lives spent in the service of the Y Bench. They rode the best horseflesh that money could buy or skill in breeding could devise.

The story of how Proctor got his start, as told by himself, has the sound of a fable; but anywhere in Texas one can hear the accepted version. In the years when cattle roamed unbranded and untended across the broad expanse of the Lone Star State just after the Civil War, young Cowles opened a slaughterhouse in Cincinnati, another in San Francisco and a third at the edge of Dallas. He did not operate these personally but put a trusted man in charge of each while he, with a gang of cowboys, rode out and corraled all the steers they could get their hands on. These, properly branded, were shipped and driven to one or another of his butcheries and there turned into meat. When mavericks began to grow scarce in Texas, he moved operation to the San Joaquin Valley in California, where the "deer and the antelope played" and cow-critters were still running plenty wild. Along this level plain, two hundred miles long by a good wide fifty across, grass grew belly-high to a horse and there was water from a mighty river. After looking this situation over, Proctor established a ranch and put his hands to work. Leaving them at it, he went over into southwestern New Mexico and opened up another, the beginnings of the present vast *La Paloma*. Grass was free and land was cheap; shrewdly Proctor bought. As fast as the money came pouring in from his slaughter shops and packing houses, he sank it in New Mexican lands. The time came when public critters free to file on began to show signs of becoming extinct. Proctor sold out two of his slaughterhouses, his packing houses, his ranch in California, and moved his outfit bag and baggage to the Sunshine State; and now, twenty years later, there was *La Paloma* to show for it—a fitting monument to any man's work.

On this particular morning he was sitting in the patio going over the accounts handed in by his superintendent the night before when Forney came in answer to a servant's call. The Y Bench super looked inquiringly at Proctor, cleared his throat a couple of times and looked a little restless when the old man paid no attention.

Proctor went on examining the accounts as though he were alone.

As time piled up and Proctor kept his super standing there like one of those fool ornaments on the fountain, Forney's face got darker and, despite the fact that he had Estrella's lovely face and neatly gowned figure to stare at, a sullen look began to smoulder in his eyes.

Cuffing his hat against a leg, he said: "Was you wantin' me, Mister Proctor?"

Cowles Proctor, still pursuing his examination, grunted testily. "In a minute—in a minute, Forney. Any reason you can't set?"

Estrella, Proctor's only daughter, concealed a smile behind her fan as Forney ungraciously yanked a chair from beside a potted yucca and deposited his gaunt body in a sprawled attitude of impatient martyrdom. The Y Bench super had always more or less amused her, at such times as nothing better offered. She found interest in his violent mannerisms, his uncouth expressions and gestures. The restless way he had of fingering his hat when her presence forced him reluctantly to remove it from his bullet head particularly amused her. She wondered idly if there'd ever been a woman in his life.

Proctor looked up suddenly, closing the account book with a snap and depositing it with the stack of others on the table.

"Well," he said, "did you see Lubbock, Forney?"

"Yeah. He ain't much interested."

Proctor's brows shot up. "Did you tell him I'd pay fifty thousand dollars for that property?"

Forney nodded sourly. "Said you'd plenty of water now. Said he wouldn't have you messin' with his canyon."

Proctor looked at him coldly, his brows drawn down and appearance of deep thought in the darkness of his faded eyes. "So he said I'd plenty of water, did he? What's he know about it? Since when's he been concernin' himself with my business! Damn old coot. What's he want to keep that water cooped for? God's sake! that river'll water a thousand acres if properly used and diverted—"

"He said," Forney butted in, "the river didn't go down that canyon—"

"He's like all them damn old desert rats—don't know nothing but followin' rainbows. Forever huntin' pots of gold that don't exist. Damn it, Bronc; I told you I wanted that canyon! Go find out what he'll take to give me title an' get the hell out of there."

Forney said: "That's just the point. He don't *want* to get out of there. He says the place is his an' he aims to keep it. Says he's filed on it legal an' has done his work accordin' to the statutes, an' that if you know what's good for you you'll tend to your cows an'—"

"Said what!"

"I told you in the beginnin'," Forney growled, "you wouldn't get no place with that coot. He's a ignorant ol' burro-chaser—stubborn as hell's own backlog, an' the more you prod him the stubborner he'll get. He's squatted on that place an'—"

"All right," Proctor said with a scowl. "Tell him he can stay there. Tell him all I want is the right to—"

"Be a waste of good time. He don't *want* you sinkin' holes in that drywash—and he don't want that canyon monkeyed with. Says it suits him just the way it is an' if you ain't satisfied with what you've got already you can lump it. In fact, he warned me off with a rifle an' said if he saw my mug aroun' there again he'd nail my hide to the fence. If you're wantin' to hunt that water, you'll have to figure some other way," Bronc Forney said, and returned Proctor's stare with as good as was sent.

"What's he got up there—a gold mine?"

"I don't know what he's got," growled Forney sullenly. "But whatever it is, he aims to keep it. I don't know a thing that you can do. He's filed on the land all right—"

"Hell, I know that! Don't you s'pose I looked it up before I sent you over to dicker?" Proctor's fingers drummed on the arms of his chair impatiently. "Must be some way round it . . . Estrella, send someone after Karvel. Mebbe he can think of something—"

"Mebbe he can shout, too," Forney muttered. He said impatiently: "What the hell can he think of I ain't already tried? The thing is this: less'n you're prepared to try open violence, there ain't—"

"Estrella—" Proctor's voice cut knifelike through the cheese of Forney's utterance "—send a *mozo* after Karvel. We'll hear what he'll have to offer, anyway."

With an amused glance at the Y Bench super, the girl strolled languidly from the patio. Forney

51

maintained a sullen silence till she returned; and that stony reserve lessened no whit when, coming back from the errand, she dropped into a chair nearby and, with a hand beneath her chin, regarded him thoughtfully.

He was a mercurial man, moody and seldom smiling. He sat with his raw-carrot cheeks tipped forward, his jaw pugnacious, and with the scarred brown hands that clamped his hat showing white about the knuckles. A strange specimen, she reflected; and one who, given sufficient encouragement, might well prove dangerous. A man to keep on one's side. A bad man to have against one.

Karvel came in with his easy smile and careless nod, scattering her thoughts as he always did. Good-looking devil. Her eyes went to his hair as he took his hat off; straight and dark it was with mahogany highlights, receding a bit on each side from his forehead. She wondered if he knew what his presence did to a woman: if he guessed what thoughts went on behind the eyes regarding him; if he understood the singing blood roused by his nearness. There was a strictly animal magnetism about him that had nothing at all to do with his good looks.

Proctor said: "Joe, what do you know about Lost Water?"

"You're talking about that underground river that swings down from the Burros and disappears south of the Seventy-Six before it hits Maverick Canyon?"

Cowles Proctor nodded.

"Well," Karvel said, "I don't know much about it. Why?"

"Ever been up around that section?"

"I expect I have. Before I went to work for the Y Bench I prospected around all through the Burros. I was huntin' tin," he said with a smile, "but all I found was a little turquoise an' a lot of low-grade iron."

"Did you prospect Maverick Canyon?"

"I poked through it."

"Nothing there, eh?"

"Well, I wouldn't want to be quoted as sayin' there wasn't. I found some pyrites. Know anyone wantin' to buy some?"

Proctor ignored his pleasantry. He said earnestly: "There's an old coot hangs out up there named Lubbock. Damn crackpot prospector. He's filed on the canyon. Ever hear of him?"

Karvel thought awhile. "Seems like there's a town of that name some place—"

"Never mind the town. I'm talkin' about this burro-chaser."

Karvel shook his head. "Don't reckon I have."

Estrella said: "Better tell him about the water, Dad."

"I'm goin' to. Look here, Joe; I've an idea that vanished river flows under that canyon. There's a drywash runnin' through it. Down there where the canyon peters out, the ground's all faulted hardpan. Years ago I think the river flowed down that wash; it's full of boulders an' stuff. But here's the dope: If the river's under there, it makes a swing to the west when it hits that faulted hardpan. All right. That's a hell of a lot of water goin' to waste—get my point? If we could find that watercourse an' turn it east—"

Karvel said dubiously: "Quite a way from our range, ain't it? Time we got it down this way flow'd be about dried up, wouldn't it?"

"Not necessarily; anyway, that part's my lookout. What I want is a chance to drill around up there, a chance to find out if I'm right. If I am, I'll find a way to get that water down here. I'd like to put in another hundred acres of alfalfa; if I could get that water I could do it."

"You say this Lubbock owns the canyon? Why not buy him out?"

"I've offered him fifty thousand dollars," Proctor growled. "The goddam fool won't sell!"

Karvel rubbed his jaw. "Kind of puts you up a stump. Give any reason?"

"Sure. I suppose you gave him my reason, didn't you?" Proctor looked at Forney.

The latter nodded. "Told him about your water scheme. Looked like he thought I was crazy or fixin' to hand him a fast one. Said somethin'

54

about it bein' contrary to nature; said if God had intended—"

"What I mean is," Karvel said, "did he give you any reason why he wouldn't sell?"

"No. He said," rapped out the Y Bench super, "that we'd got enough water now, an' that if he caught me sneakin' round the place again, he'd fill me so full of lead it'd make a sieve look solid by comparison." He scowled. "My advice is to let that jigger plumb alone—"

"Your advice wasn't asked for." Proctor looked at Karvel. "What do you think, Joe? Any way to get around him?"

Karvel looked at the super quizzically, rubbing a reflective hand across his jaw. That jaw showed the steel in him; belying the easy-going humor to be read in the almond-shaped eyes that sized up men and situations with the same tolerant indifference—with the same mind-your-own-business way of suspending judgment.

"I dunno," he answered finally, looking back at Proctor. "Require a bit of headwork. Might be able to dream up something. How long can I have?"

"Till this time tomorrow. Lay off for the rest of the day an' put your mind to it," Proctor grunted. "An' for the Lord's sake think of something. I got to have that water."

55

Chapter 7

IN THE CAVERN

During the next few days following the girl's refusal to give him meat, Rush Rago, flat on his back in the lumpy bunk, did a lot of thinking. But it didn't seem to get him any place. Somehow the girl's covert looks at him seemed to imply a longer acquaintance than his occupancy of the bunk could warrant. Too, there was a familiarity in some of her mannerisms that gave him a feeling of having known her prior to his painful awakening in the shack. But he could not place her; even now he did not know her name. Nor did he know the identity of the lank stoop-shouldered man with the hollowed cheeks and ragged mustache he sometimes saw about the place— mainly during breakfast and supper—save that he was this girl's father; at least she called him "Paw" and he, in turn, addressed her gruffly as "daughter."

Such a circumstance was surely sufficiently embarrassing. To be the recipient of a reluctant hospitality—and it *was* reluctant if the old man's sly, suspicious glances and the girl's odd looks and close-mouthed reticence were taken into account—without knowing what he had done to incur this silent resentment was distinctly annoying. But he supposed he could have borne it equably if that had been all. It wasn't. He didn't even know his own name—couldn't to save his blessed life recall it or his reason for being there or how he had come by this gunshot wound! And he could get no help whatever from the girl; if her expressions could be relied on, at such times as he brought it up, she plainly didn't believe him, was convinced it was a pose he was adopting to further some dark end.

For hours he struggled with these problems. Other hours, defeated, brooding, he lay restless on his hard bed awaiting the girl's return. She was out of the house for long stretches at a time; not far away, though, for occasionally he could hear her moving about outside some place, and twice he heard her humming fragments of some half-remembered song.

When she came inside he lay back easier, watching her moving about her work, dusting, putting things to order, sweeping the bare earth floor. She used a spruce branch for this project, and her employment of it revealed her lithe, slim figure admirably; revealed it and roused in him an unsuspected hunger that made him more than ever restless after she went out.

She never stayed long, seeming to hurry her work, attacking it sometimes with a vigor that was surprising. He had commented on this one time and got a scowl from her flushed face that should have withered him; but he had chuckled, making complimentary twaddle concerning her good looks.

He liked the strange dark pride descried in the tilt of lifted chin; her courageous spirit. There were sufficient contradictions in her makeup so that a man could think of her all day long yet never quite manage to figure her out. She had, he thought, the shyness of an antelope, and that animal's curiosity. And somehow he got the idea she was nursing a secret longing for better things than she had known. It was not from anything she said; it was just that oddly wistful shadow caught now and again far back in the depths of those strangely expressive eyes. Her lot was not an easy one; darned few girls, he guessed, would be willing to spend their lives as hers was spent garbed in some man's cast-off garments, in a box-wood shack way back in the hills this way.

He wondered what she found to do—what that gruff old sinner she addressed as "Paw" did, away so much of his time. A prospector, probably. It kind of seemed as if he'd been a prospector once himself; there was a familiar sort of ring to the word. He turned it over on his tongue and grimaced. His mind had sure gone back on him. It was a damn sad case when a man couldn't tell either his own name or his business!

He struggled with the mystery of his being there for an exasperating couple of hours and then, without enlightenment, slept.

The days passed slowly, constrained as he was by orders and his own condition to lie upon this ungiving bunk with nothing but his thoughts for company. Some would have called it the life of Riley, but Rago didn't deem it that. He was impatient to be up and about, to do things with his hands and give his confounded mind a rest. The girl's name, he had learned at last, was Clementine—but that was about all he *had* learned about her.

She still appeared to regard him with that intriguing admixture of shy curiosity and dark suspicion that had marked her from the first. And she still maintained that stubborn reticence. The inexplicable shadow, too, continued to be visible in her glances when she looked in his direction. It were as though they shared some secret best not put into words. But she *had* got round to talking with him. As long as he kept the conversation impersonal they got along like old school friends, but let him so much as hint at matters puzzling him and talk would die on the instant.

It was uncanny. A definite curtain was steadily drawn on things pertaining to the locality, to the old man's work, to himself, his wound, and to his reason for being here. Anything else was fine and dandy, but these things were taboo; they were *shh-shh* subjects and not to be mentioned if you cared to indulge in tongue-wagging.

He was getting heartier grub now, and the day came finally when he was permitted to sit up. Two days of this and she allowed him to hobble about the cabin briefly; not that he had any particular need of hobbling, but he must, she said, take care of himself—he was weak and had to take things easy. The idea, he thought resentfully, obviously being that the quicker he was fully recovered and out of there the better they'd be satisfied. They wanted no relapses—nothing must happen that by any stretch of the imagination might delay his approaching departure.

The first thing he did when he got on his feet was to make for the shack's one window. But she kept him away from there with the threat of putting him back to bed. She said that was too far for him to walk; that he might get dizzy or faint or something and then what would she do?

So he sat in a chair and glowered. Occasionally he got up and walked about the far side of the room. That was all right, he guessed; he wouldn't get dizzy there!

"In a few days now you'll be as good as new," she said. "I allow you'll be plumb glad to git back home again, won't you? Expect your wife must think you are dead, you been away so long."

He glared, then grinned at her lopsidedly. "I

ain't married—thank God," he said. "I can still do what I please with my time."

It kind of made him riled the way they were so damn anxious to get rid of him; made him do considerable speculating, too. Fellow'd think he was a leper, the way they acted. And all this secrecy! He wondered if he'd made some kind of pass at her or something.

But the next day she said he could sit outside a bit if he'd mind and do what she told him. He promised promptly—he'd have promised anything to get outside for a bit. But when he got there he was disappointed. He didn't recognize the landscape at all. This shack, he found, was in the face of a red rock cliff; it looked down upon a wide and empty canyon that sweltered in the sun and had a drywash running through the middle of it. A barren, uninviting sort of place which was entered from this cliff cave by a narrow, pick-chipped path that twisted dangerously down the wall, a trail not even a goat would tackle with impunity.

He looked at her inquiringly. She said, "Nice view, ain't it?" He looked again and grunted some unintelligible reply. Then after a time he said, "Be a good place to hole up if a guy was hiding out."

She let that pass as if she hadn't heard it. She put a hand upon his shoulder. "Don't get so near the edge. You might get sick and fall."

Rush Rago snorted. But he got back as she told him, sitting down beside her in the shadow of the cave. He eyed the Sharps that leaned by her hand against the wall. "Ever see anything to shoot at?"

She looked at him queerly, a dark light shading the edges of her eyes. But she didn't bother speaking. She was like that; like an Indian. She didn't seem to have much use for words.

He guessed she got that way from living so long alone out here with her Paw. Might's well talk at a cliff as to try and carry on a conversation with *him*. He didn't see how she stood it. "Must get pretty lonesome up here for you."

"There's folks," she said, "as cottons to bein' lonesome."

"Mean to say if you had your way you wouldn't go live in some town? Wouldn't you like to fool around with other girls, have nice fancy things to wear an' have the boys come sparkin'—?"

"Sparkin'? What's that?"

Rush got a little red and scowled. "Ain't no fellas ever wanted to keep you company?"

"Ain't no fellas around here—not that I'd let 'em if there was." She looked at him curiously for a moment, kind of searching like. "What does a fella do when he keeps comp'ny with a girl?"

"Why—uh—" Rush stared at his boots as if he expected to find the answer written on them. "Hell! he slicks up some, I suppose, an' puts in as much of his time with her as her old man will let him."

"Well, what's he do when he's with her?"

"Makes her pretty speeches—"

"What's the good of that?"

"Hell, I dunno." Rush scowled at the .30-.30, wishing he hadn't started this conversation. It sounded as if she were fixing to have some fun with him. It didn't seem possible she really didn't know anything about such matters. Of course, living way back in the hills this way—

"Go on; tell me some more about it. What else does he do?"

"Holds her hand, I guess, if the girl don't raise a rumpus. Mebbe tells her how much better things'd be if they could get hitched up—"

"Hitched up to what?"

Rush looked at her intently, shook his head and muttered: "Married. That's just a way of sayin' it."

She said: "I guess you ain't done much of it, have you? What's he do after that?"

"Depends on the girl, I reckon."

"You mean if she likes it? If she does, does he grab aholt of her an'—" she glared at the ground—"an' kinda wrassle with her an'—"

"Not if he's any kind of—I mean, not if his intentions is good ones," Rush said gruffly.

"Oh. Well, what *does* he do?"

"Hell, I dunno. Kisses her, I reckon, an'

lovey-dovey's round." He quit talking irritably and glared at the .30-.30. This was a hell of a conversation. How did *he* know what they did? He'd never had any time for that kind of foolishness himself; had always been too busy with one thing and another.

He stiffened. What the hell *had* he been so busy at? He wished to God he could remember who he was!

She didn't seem to notice his abstraction. She was staring down at her bare feet as if she were concentrating on something. One big toe was nudging a pebble along toward a place where further nudging would shove it off into the canyon. She said consideringly: "Guess you'd kinda like to spark *me,* if I was willin', wouldn't you?"

Rush went cold and hot all over; stared at her suspiciously. But she was looking off down the canyon and he couldn't make out much of her expression. It seemed kind of dreamy-like. Damned if he didn't believe she was in earnest, at that!

She wouldn't be hard to look at—even for the rest of a fellow's life. But memory of the old man's squinched-up eyes was much too plain. And that dour, suspicious mouth with its unpleasant habit of slyly leering when a fellow least expected it. He didn't want to have to look at that across no table for the rest of his natural life.

She had turned, the blue of her eyes gone dark and sort of swimmy. The flaming red of lips and hair made pulse-stirring contrast with the cool, tan oval of her face. Rush felt his blood start singing and an excited prickling got to racing up and down his spine.

But he managed to keep himself in hand. "I guess most any gent would . . ."

A thoughtful, kind of inquiring look was cutting faint lines between her eyes; and the eyes themselves were changing. He could see surprise in the glance she threw him. "I ain't interested in ' 'most any gent'—I'm askin' about *you*."

Rush didn't like that edge of challenge in her glance. He didn't like her direct way of pressing him for an answer, either. The crushed-berry redness of her lips was very close. He wished she wouldn't sit so near. It wasn't that she were not desirable. She was—he guessed bee trees would be like gall beside her. But hell! He didn't want no truck with a woman. If it came to that, who could say but that he was already tied to some dame's apron strings? He wished the hell he could remember.

He woke up suddenly to the change that had taken place in her watching features. In the blue of her gaze, cold sparks were glinting; her tightened cheeks showed resentful color. There was mingled anger and malice in the long hard look she gave him.

"Guess I been kinda runnin' off at the mouth. You look plumb tuckered, stranger. Reckon it's time you was gettin' back to bed again—don't want you takin' on no fever."

She came erect and, picking up the rifle, motioned him to his feet. No need of her stormy eyes to tell him what a fool he'd been. On sudden impulse he grabbed her, pulled her to him and kissed her full upon the lips.

The reaction was like spiked tequila; he felt it clear to his boot heels. With the whole world reeling, rocking, crashing, he put his mouth to hers again. He heard the fall of her rifle and for one wild singing instant he felt response rushing through her. Then she was fighting; with all the fierce, crazed strength of a wildcat she was striving to break his hold, pounding him with her fists. Her clawed fingers were tearing through his hair; she was panting, squirming, writhing.

Something struck him across the eyes and he let go, reeling back against the cavern wall, groping for a handhold blindly lest he stagger across the brink and plunge to the canyon rocks below.

He heard the slap of running feet, the receding pant of her labored breathing; and then, wiping the water from his burning eyes, he saw her, rifle forgotten, far below. She was like an antelope, her bare feet flashing along that treacherous trail, spurning the danger of its narrow twistings, seeking only to escape his reach; angry, frightened, humiliated, sobbing as she ran.

There was a pain in his side and his watering eyes hurt cruelly, but his blood still throbbed at the recollection of their contact. There was a wild elation in him, filling him with a pagan joy. He'd never guessed a kiss could do that to him. He was not at all regretful for his actions; not very regretful, anyway. It had been worth it. But he'd have to get out of there. She was mad—she was as mad as hops, and when the old man came back he'd be mad too. He'd probably want a shotgun wedding if he didn't kill Rush out of hand.

Rush dragged a sleeve across his eyes and went inside the shack. His gun was around there some place. He didn't recall seeing it round any place, but he wasn't going off without it. He looked around. The cupboard—that's where she'd put it.

He commenced rummaging.

But it wasn't there.

He looked under the bunk but didn't find it among the odds and ends stuffed there, either. He went to the door that was always kept closed beneath the antlers. That was where the girl slept nights; she always went through that door when she went to bed.

He pulled it open; with a muttered imprecation dived back hunting a match. It was as black as hell back there. He remembered seeing matches in the cupboard. He went back, caught up a handful, struck one.

There was a room all right. It was to the left with a door in the soapbox facing. But it was something else that caught Rush's eye. The cavern, contrary to his expectations, didn't end there. It went on back, stretching away in a narrowed passage as far as his matchlight penetrated. He recalled now it was through this door the old man vanished every morning— through this door the old man came at night.

Then his glance fell on two bulging sacks.

He dropped the burnt-out match and struck another; a fever of excitement pulsing through his veins like fire. He forgot the girl—forgot the reason for his being there. With the match in a cupped left hand, he bent and with his right hand tore the fastening from the neck of the nearest gunnysack and pulled it open. Hunkered stiffly in his haunches, he crouched there, staring, his bright eyes wide, incredulous.

He was like that, his jaw sagging, when a faint scream knifed the silence.

Chapter 8

IN THE CANYON

Overwhelmed by panic, breaking free of Rago's grip, the girl rushed blindly from the cavern. She was like a rope-scared colt, without reason, with no recourse to logic, knowing but the one intense desire—escape. She burst from the cave-mouth's gloom into the gold bright gush of sunlight without pause or heed for natural dangers. Sobbing, panting, beside herself with terror, she went bolting down the crazy trail that clung with such precariousness to the sheer, high cliffs.

She made it—made the canyon floor in safety; darted a quick and harried look across her shoulder. She more than half expected to find him right behind; to see his hand outstretched, his mouth spread in a gloating grin. But he wasn't there. She heard nothing but the roaring clamor of her heart against her ribs.

He wasn't coming then! Or was this but a ruse to quiet her fears? A shift to lull her into false security?

She ran again, sped on until, panting, exhausted, unable to run farther, she reached the big rock behind which he had hidden the day she had shot him, and behind the sanctuary of its barrier sprawled face down in the sand, horror thick upon her.

It was not so much the man himself she feared as contact—contact with an alien body, and all the tumult such a contact roused. She could not bear to touch or be touched; the very thought brought out a sweat of terror. She did not seek to find the reason for this madness; she only knew that to feel another's hands upon her filled her with unbearable loathing and disgust.

Reaction from that scene with Rago left her trembling in every limb, left her nerves stretched taut and screaming, left her cowering in nameless fear. That he should dare take hold of her! Dare put his mouth on hers! She wished, she told herself vehemently, she had killed him!

The torment in her eased a little then; gradually the fierce tumult of outraged emotions quieted. She felt weaker than a kitten. Used up and limp, she sprawled outstretched upon the sand with the sun beating warmly on her. For a long time she lay there, voiceless and unmoving; unthinking. She lay there till her breath came back, till her jerking nerves relaxed and the flutter left her heart.

She got up then and cuffed the sand from her clothing. Resentment still burned strong in her and she felt unclean, still soiled by the stranger's touch. She sought out a little pool she knew in a tiny gulch that opened off the canyon and, scooping up the cleansing water in cupped palms, scrubbed out her mouth and spat and gargled, and washed her face and neck with such determined vigor as to leave them pink and glowing.

All men were alike, she told herself, and cursed them for a pack of grinning, grasping brutes. To think she'd felt regret for shooting one filled her with a hot contempt. It was too damn bad she hadn't killed him! By God, she *would* if he tried touching her again! She clenched her fists and bit her lip in shame as she recalled the pity she had felt for him while he lay helpless in her bunk.

What a fool she'd been to nurse him back to health! It was just like in the Bible—like that girl who'd cuddled the viper! She ought to have had more sense!

A viper—that's what he was. A sneaking, belly-crawling snake in the grass; an unregenerate, ungrateful human skunk, lifting his head to bite the hand that fed him!

How was she going to face Paw with that reptile's kiss still on her mouth? She could feel Paw's sly, accusing eyes upon her now. She knew she could never face him; he'd know in that dour, quiet way of his what had happened as soon as he saw her. He had a name for women who let men do that to them; he'd read her about them plenty from the Good Book—Jezebels, he called them; and she hung her head in shame.

She looked down into the water bitterly, half

expecting to see the stranger's kiss on her face like a brand. She guessed she'd have to tell Paw. He'd find it out anyway. And he always said the truth was best no matter how it hurt.

Maybe he'd forgive her, this time. But sure as hell she'd be in for a lot of reading. It was mortal strange, she thought, what an uncommon amount the Good Book had to say about her kind of woman. It seemed as if in the old days most of the women had been right ornery—what time they weren't begetting. She wondered with a new alarm if the stranger's kiss were going to have that effect, and her cheeks got hot as fire. Might be she ought to take a wash all over . . . Maybe if she scrubbed herself enough and said a few good prayers—

She had got that far in her reflections, and her hands were reaching tentatively to the buttons of her shirt, when the sound of a bootstep whirled her.

She took one look and screamed.

Chapter 9

DARK FANCIES

Les Durango, during the course of his career, had been many things to many men. He had been a sheep rustler over near Hackberry Basin after saying goodbye to his father's old red schoolhouse; and when the Basin country had become too hot to hold him, he had migrated to Gagsby Creek, Texas, where he began a practice of doctoring cattle. This occupation was cut short one evening when he was caught red-handed by the brothers who owned the animals. Leaving both men where they fell, he got astride his caballo and rolled his hocks for other parts. Next time he got in the limelight was over at Tombstone with a deputy's job under Wyatt Earp. Three masked hombres stepped into the Crystal Palace while he was playing draw poker with a couple of visiting brand inspectors; carefully laying his cards and cigar on an edge of the table, he jerked both pistols without wasting time in argument and let drive, killing two of the would-be robbers on the instant and nicking the third, who departed dripping blood. Putting the cigar in his mouth and picking up his cards, Durango had resumed the game without comment. Impressed witnesses hastened to spread the news and, as a result, three weeks later he was offered a marshal's star at Silver City. Trouble with a parson's daughter cut short his stay at Silver. Never the man to linger where he wasn't wanted, he departed posthaste for his cousin's diggings at Cripple Creek. There he dropped from sight for a while, having learned no doubt to cover his tracks to better advantage.

Eight years later he was back in the public eye with a bang, having made the front pages of every important paper in Texas in connection with a particularly malignant killing just outside the town limits of El Paso. An old man, later discovered to be an important rancher in the Black Range country, was found dead one noon at the edge of the desert. The return half of a train ticket in his pocket served to clinch the identification of the victim when the local sheriff on a hunch wired Silver City. Investigation showed that the rancher, getting off the train that morning at El Paso, had been met by Durango and two other gents in a rented car. Apparently the old man had come down for the express purpose of contacting them, Durango having earlier been up in the Black Range country under the guise of being in the market for a ranch. He had visited the ranchman, looked over his property and expressed himself satisfied that things were as specified, and had arranged for the old man to come to El Paso for completion of the deal. When arrested, Durango was found to have ten thousand dollars in big bills on his person. At the ensuing trial Durango admitted killing the man, but said he was acting as hired-gun hombre for another party who had paid him the ten thousand for putting a window in the old man's skull. As to the identity of his two companions in the rented car, Durango kept a hobbled jaw, and no amount of legal browbeating was able to make him loosen up. He was sentenced to six years' hard labor in the pen; but was paroled after serving two.

Nothing more was heard of him for twelve years. Either he'd gone into hiding, folks said, or some one of his didos had caught up with him and he'd been polished off with some of his own damn medicine.

This was proved to have been mostly wishful thinking. In 1912 he made another public appearance, this time in the role of Good Samaritan, when he saved the life of Archie Jandsen, eccentric millionaire, who'd been snake-bitten while prospecting the copper country in the neighborhood of Bisbee. The grateful Easterner, sure Durango's heroic remedies had saved him from a terrible death, had placed twenty-five thousand dollars to his credit in a Tucson bank.

For the next two years the rambler lived upon the fat of the land; surrounded by fair-weather friends and a veritable host of retainers, his carryings-on and prodigal parties earned him an envious place in the gossip columns of the West Coast papers. He was the friend of capitalists, the boon companion of international celebrities.

Then, suddenly, the last of his twenty-five thousand was gone—and so were his friends and companions. But Durango, with his now familiar scowl, took good and bad luck alike. With his last few shekels he threw a rip-roaring party for the press. When everyone was feeling at his peak, the wine flowing freely and the girls becoming intimate, Durango made his farewell speech. He was going, he said, back to the desert that had bred and nurtured him; back to the first of his occupations—prospecting. He was going to hunt for gold.

He went, and the West Coast heard no more of him.

But he'd no more intention of prospecting than had the man in the moon. He was playing another of his hunches, and it took him into the Little Burros above Tyrone, east of the Seventy-Six, where he fell in with a prospector named Lubbock, who'd been born in St. Louis a good many years before. Mention Ed Gable and Missourians would understand *muy pronto* whom you had in mind; Gable had achieved fierce notoriety some eighteen years back for the killing of an influential apostate Mormon at Joplin. Gable had departed through a hail of lead and without any qualms concerning whose horse he took to do it. Two months later the Mormon's widow, having disposed quite profitably of the dead man's estates and chattels, had also shaken the dust of Joplin from her high French heels. She left a lot of tongue-wagging in her wake but no forwarding address, and it was popularly supposed that she had gone to join Gable.

Lubbock had no woman, but he had a daughter, Clementine, whose probable age was about eighteen. Durango took a good long look at her and grinned. The next time he and Lubbock were alone they had quite a talk, Durango doing the prompting and the old prospector, for the most part, answering in surly monosyllables save for the one or two times he raised his voice with an ugly look in his eye. But Durango was accustomed to hard looks and had an answer for every scowl. When he departed a short time later, there was a bulging poke lashed fast to his saddlebow and he said: "So long," with a knowing grin.

When the Burro Mountain crowd decided to invest in Tyrone copper, took over the old Chemunga diggings and started opening up some new ones, it was determined to make the camp a model town. This called for landscaping, uniform architecture, and ordinances; it called for political machinery. It called particularly for a town marshal, for there were some hard characters forting up in the hills. The Company sent out notice of their needs, dumped seventeen million in the pot for construction and development, and began interviewing applicants for the marshal's job. One man appeared to stand head and shoulders above all comers. He had kicked down more damn doors and gone through a sight more powder smoke after things he'd set his mind on than all the rest of them put together—and they didn't have to take his word for it. He was a low talker, an easy smiler, a good mingler and a fellow who could get along without smoking, drinking, or gambling, though he'd done all three in his time. He was, in his way, a kind of minor celebrity and was on back-slapping terms with a lot of the West Coast prominent. These were solid virtues, and without resorting to bluster he made no denial that he'd been in trouble with various authorities a number of times. The man who talked to him was especially impressed with the fact that he made no protestations of false regret. "He stood," this official told the board, "right up on his hind feet an' looked me squarely in the eye. He's the very man we need, boys—with a .45-.60 he's a sure shot up to a mile, and with his rep there ain't nobody going to try putting anything over on him, believe you me. The job'll be a sinecure for him an' as long as he toes the mark. I, for one, say we can't find better if we hunt the whole damn West."

So Durango with his two guns, his sloe-eyed reticence, his pockmarked face of parboiled leather and his memories, became Tyrone's first marshal.

It was a job that suited him well, being endowed not only with a good many possibilities, but with the added attraction of keeping him close to Lubbock, and the stuff Lubbock put in his gunnysacks.

Life had been a bowl of cherries the first few months of this project, the Company's pay being amplified by diverse other incomes Durango felt no call to explain. Seldom did "Justice Court"— as the adobe-and-plaster jail was called—have inhabitants, and even upon such far apart occasions the inmate was only a loud carouser, incarcerated to sleep it off.

But with Haigler's coming things had changed. Durango's carefree, easygoing existence had taken a new and disquieting turn. He was not so young as he had been, and the leisured, affluent life of these last few years had put him in a state of mind where trifles of a certain sort were apt to stick in his craw. He was, perhaps, no more sensitive to atmospheres than the next, but Haigler and himself appeared to have conceived a dislike for each other on sight. This was in no way minimized when, as Kurt Ruddabaugh introduced them, Crow-Rondack's man had said: "Marshal—?" and flipped his eyebrows up.

It might have ended there had not Durango chanced to overhear that Haigler was evincing an interest in the Y Bench's foreman and super. He deemed that something to look into and forthwith peeled his eyes for evidence which, to a man of the marshal's abilities, was not a great while forthcoming. They were, as he'd told Ruddabaugh, "thicker'n fiddlers in hell." He had read a book quite recently which gave him a very apt title which he rolled off his tongue with zest. The "Unholy Three" was what he called them, and hoped to hell they'd hear of it.

His animosity would not have taken so quick a turn had Haigler shown signs of being reasonable. Actually he'd been downright offensive. After five days of surveillance, conjecture and brooding, Durango had met Phil Haigler on the street one morning and put it to him, man to man.

"You an' them Y Bench boys are up to something," he remarked, and rubbed the back of his neck while he looked at Haigler knowingly. "How much you payin' me to keep it dark?"

Crow-Rondack's man regarded him with a granite stare, abruptly stretching his face around a contemptuous laugh. He was wheeling, starting off, when Durango grabbed his arm. "Just a minute, friend. Happens I'm the law in this man's town . . ."

"What of it?"

"Just this." Durango held his temper with an

effort. "You an' Forney an' Karvel been doin' a heap of gassin' with your heads together. You been ridin' the hills; been meetin' each other in damn queer places—"

"No law against it, is there?"

"You're missin' the point, friend. *I'm* the law." He paused, giving the idea time to get across, then said: "If I was to go to Proctor—"

"You can go to Halifax for all of me," Haigler said, and turned on his heel.

But the marshal wasn't done. "Hold on!" he scowled. "You better listen. You an' them Y Benchers may be feelin' pretty slick, but you ain't pullin' no wool over *my* eyes. I'm warnin' you—first crooked move I catch onto's goin' to book you for the can!"

Haigler laughed and walked off, leaving him standing there.

But Durango was not the kind of man to pull that stuff with. He had a dexterity born of his needs and a high suspicion which he kept honed like a razor. Looking after Haigler, his stubbornness showed in the forward thrust of his chin, in the tight-clamped line of his leathery lips.

A soft call reached out, the urgency of it fighting its way through his absorption, wheeling him round and pulling him toward the black-smith shop at a long stride. A rider sat his horse just inside the open doorway. He was a heavy, formless shape in that shaded gloom, but Durango knew him. He said quickly, irritably:

"I told you where you could leave a message. I told you—"

"I figured you wouldn't be wantin' this dope to cool," said Buck Tooth Bransen, grinning. "I cut sign on them fellas this time. Up in the Burros. Follered 'em clean on up into Willow Creek Canyon where the sign give out in the water. Tracks was headin' north when I lost 'em." He looked at the marshal significantly. "I figured you'd want to know."

"Headin' north, eh?" Durango nodded. He said through curled-back lips: "How old was them tracks, Bransen?"

"Two-three days."

"Can't you put it closer'n that?"

The rider shrugged. "I reckon you hired me account of me bein' the bes' damn tracker you could get."

"All right." Durango rolled his shoulders. "Forget them Y Benchers. I want you to keep your glimmers peeled on Haigler. Any time he leaves town, you foller him. An', by God, see to it you don't lose him. I want to know where he goes an' what he does." He handed the man a roll of bills and left the place without further words just as the blacksmith entered.

Back in his office, Durango's pockmarked face went dark and ugly, showing the twisting of his thoughts, showing the bitter suspicion that was in him. They had been prowling through Willow Creek Canyon, had they? He clenched his fists till their knuckles gleamed bright as snow, and the fury roused by Bransen's report glittered with a cold malevolence through the slits of his hooded eyes.

Going north, the tracker'd said. Damn them! There was only one place they could go in that direction—Maverick Canyon. It was where Ed Gable hung out.

Chapter 10

A PLEASANT PROSPECT

That scream cut short Rush's amazement, drove through his abstraction like a flint-tipped arrow and brought him up on his boot heels; startled, intent, straining his ears against the far dim gurgle of hidden waters.

A full minute passed unmarked by further event. Sure that the scream had come from the girl, Rush's first thought had been that a snake had struck her; there were always snakes in these rocky canyons. But now Rush wasn't so sure. If it had been a snake she could have screamed again. Yet what else could have scared her?

With a worried curse he shoved the gunnysack back in its corner and hurried out into the cabin. But she wasn't there; the place was empty. If she hadn't returned she must still be down in the canyon.

Girls were like that he thought; always bothering a man—always rilin' a fellow up when he least cared to be interrupted. But she might be hurt—might have fallen or something.

He hurried outside and from the cave-mouth scoured the canyon floor below, but without sign of her.

Really worried now, he grabbed up the .30-.30 and started down the trail. Narrow as a goat track, insecure as spider's web, it clung precariously to the sheer red cliff, a treacherous foothold with the rocks of the canyon floor leering up at him as though defying him to traverse it.

But the girl had used it. He had seen her speeding down it in the grip of anger, heedless of its dangers, her flying feet making mockery of its patent insecurities. He would never admit that any mere girl could do a thing too brash for him.

He went on, hurrying his pace a bit, crawling across the dizzying heights, trotting along the less fearful places, working gradually lower till at last he reached the welcome safety of the dry-wash's rock-littered bed.

He cast about for sign; saw the mark of her naked feet at once and followed them to where she'd thrown herself face down behind a huge red boulder. It looked as if she'd stayed there quite a spell—five-ten minutes, anyway. Then she'd got to her feet as though hurried by some decision and gone off down the canyon.

He followed her tracks, losing them, rediscovering them farther on. They led him off through a side canyon scuffed by horse tracks to a little pool in the shade of an alder thicket. He had kept a sharp lookout coming in and had seen no sign of her tracks coming out—yet she was not there.

He stiffened, staring sharply as a pungent exclamation crossed his lips. Bending, he crouched tensely above the red, tracked mud of the pool. He scanned the sign with narrowed stare and with a quick breath cursed as the meaning of it grabbed him. The girl had been there—bathing, probably—when someone had come up behind her. Suddenly, at the last moment, something had betrayed him. The girl had whirled, had seen him—screamed; but despite resistance had been swiftly overpowered.

It was all there, beaten in the red mud round the pool; kicked and stamped deep into it by the bitter, desperate swings of surging bodies.

Yet, fast as it had been in starting, the fight had ended just as quickly. Rush could see where the man had grabbed her, lurched her up and off her feet—where, with her locked and struggling in his arms, he'd staggered to his horse. There, frantic, she had more than doubled the wild fury of her struggles; but he had made the saddle with her.

Rush followed the horse's clear tracks in a circle to the left; the sign swung then, returning directly to the canyon. Rush, following it that far, came jarring to a sudden stop.

Waiting squarely in the trail stood Paw.

There was a cold grin on his lips, and it wasn't pleasant. Nor was there anything approaching pleasantry in the way his right hand hung beside his belt. The butt of a pistol was under that hand, and the narrowed, faded eyes held a hot and jerky look.

He said: "Where is she?"

There was sweat on Rago's cheeks; a film of it was on his neck and on the backs of his hands. He read the danger which lay in this man instantly; measured it by the stillness of Paw's attention, by the bright and suspicious smouldering of his eyes—in the malicious forward tilting of his body.

"That habit's goin' to get you into trouble sometime," Rush said quietly.

There was no change visible in the set of Paw's tight features. The hollow cheeks stayed just as stiff, the thin smile just as grimacing. "What habit?"

"That one you got of jumpin' to conclusions—"

"Don't waste any more time, stranger. I don't like you anyway an' 'ud jest as lief put a hole in you as not. Where is she? What've you done with her?"

It stirred Rush Rago's temper; made him furiously, uncaringly angry. "You're too damn free with your tongue for me—too damn free by far. How do I know where she is? 'F you're so rip-roarin' smart, suppose you find her."

Paw's spare, lank shape leaned lower. He said with a wicked calm: "If she'd done what I told her an' let you croak, this wouldn'ta happened."

He stared at Rago bitterly. "Ain't too late to croak you yet. Talk quick. You know where she is or you wouldn't be packin' that rifle."

"If it comes to that," Rush said, "where have *you* been? 'F you'd stick round once in a while like you ought to, you'd have heard her scream—"

"I heard her—"

"That," Rush growled, "is when I picked up the rifle. She'd gone down into the canyon here some place an' I'd gone back inside. When I heard her holler, I grabbed up the rifle an' come down here."

Paw's thin lips pressed together. His gaunt face showed an edge of fear. Rush caught that look and marked it, saying more easily: "Come back here in the gulch a piece. Whoever grabbed her jumped her there—I'll show you."

Without speaking, with his hand still close to the butt of his pistol, Paw followed him. Rush took him to the pool and pointed out the tracks. "Guess you can read them, can't you? You can see where she was standin'—here. See there—that's where he was creepin' up on her. This place is where he grabbed her. See the way that ground is scuffed up there? She musta fought like hell; but he got her into the saddle—see?"

"I been through the first grade," Paw said with a hard look. "I kin savvy all that stuff. But that don't mean it wasn't you—"

"Well, goddam!" Rush said and, scowling, stamped a boot beside the fellow's track. "Does that look like mine?"

Paw looked at it reluctantly. Unconvinced, he growled, "You smell like a goddam Y Bench hand to me," and wrapped a gnarled fist round his pistol.

Rush ignored it. He stared at the man, exasperated. "I don't even know the brand—never heard of it. While you're doin' all this jawin'—"

Paw said: "Pick up that rifle. We'll settle this thing right now."

"How settle it?"

"We're goin' to foller that hoss."

"On foot?"

"You don't see no ridin' gear around here, do you? Go on—lead off."

Rush looked at him. "I suppose you know that skunk may be layin' an ambush? That trackin' him this way will prob'ly walk us right smack into it?"

A thin grin licked Paw's lips. "That'll be tough—" he said "—on you."

Chapter 11

"JUST LET HIM DRAW IT!"

Rush had read the sign aright. Clementine had been standing with her face swung toward the pool, hands reaching for the buttons of her shirt, when that unexpected sound had turned her. The upper portion of a man's body showed through the screening alder; he was hardly three feet off, chest slanted, one arm raised in the act of parting the intervening foliage.

She understood her danger instantly. The crouching posture of his body, the stealth with which he'd staked her, his glinting eyes, the shaping of his full red lips all warned her of his purpose. With an involuntary scream she turned and fled.

On she ran, stumbling over rocks and brush, fright and terror obscuring her vision, threat of another contact within so short a space completely unnerving her, giving her no chance for collected thinking, dethroning reason utterly, leaving her prey to a blind and headlong panic. All she could see or sense were those reaching, claw-like hands, that too red mouth, the beady, gleaming eyes.

A lunging hand caught her shoulder and she

heard his grunt of triumph. She nearly fainted from the shock of contact; then all that rough grasp heralded served to rouse her—became a spur to her resistance.

She wrenched herself away. But almost instantly the hand caught hold of her shirt. She felt it give and struggled frantically to put herself beyond his reach. But without avail. He was like a demon—like something from a nightmare. She could feel the pulse of his fetid breath.

Sick with horror, shuddering with shock and fear, she reached a cedar stump and clung to it with all the desperate misery with which a drowning man grabs wildly at a straw. She could run no more. She leaned there limply, trembling. She was caught—like the rabbit in the deadfall in that terrible, final moment before the dropping rock crushes out its last fluttering spark of life. All hope was gone. Black terror had turned her blood to water, had weighted her limbs with lead. She crouched there paralyzed, trapped, eyes staring fixedly at the leering brute who had made himself her master.

A fragment of her shirt still hung in tatters from his hand. As though becoming that moment aware of it, he dropped it, raising the hand to his bristly jaw; gloating as his searing glance burned into her bare shoulder.

When she recovered enough to breathe without that racking whistle, she saw him starting toward her. She cowered against the stump, mute, with frightened eyes wildly pleading.

"Shucks, girl. I ain't goin' to hurt you none. Buck up."

But the look of him was not so reassuring. That gleam still marked his gaze; it scorched her, boring through her clothes and baring the very soul of her. She whispered, shuddering: "What—what is it you want with me?"

"Just want to take you for a ride," he said. "See—even brought my horse along. That's him—right over there. Best cuttin' out horse in the state."

But she wasn't listening. One word of his struck through her, bringing fresh fears, adding new terror to the old. She shrank from his reaching hand, from his purpose, from the look that was in his eyes.

"I don't want to go—I want to stay right here—"

"Shucks, you'll never get no place back in these hills. Girl like you oughta be in a city. Come on now; I ain't goin' to hurt you. Never fight the bridle, I always say. Don't get you no place an' only wastes a man's time."

She eluded his outstretched hand, and his smile. He scowled. "Now look here, girl. I ain't no man to fool with. I got a chore to do an' aim to do it—whether it suits your book or not. Get over there an' climb into that saddle."

"No," she said, and shook her head at him. "No."

"An' by God I say yes!" He took a great step forward. "You goin' to get in that saddle or am I goin' t' put you in it?"

She put the stump between them, and the fellow cursed. "By God, we'll see!" he said, and jumped for her.

She tried to get away, but he was too fast. He caught her roughly round the waist and swung her off her feet. She pounded her fists against his face, knocked his hat off, pulled his hair. Such antics seemed to amuse him, for he laughed; and with some unintelligible expression from the cow camps carried her bodily toward his horse.

But some of the dread wore away, or, perhaps, it was her natural courage reviving. When he tried to put her in the saddle, she fought him with a renewed energy, scratching at him, kicking him, writhing, twisting, striking. His cheeks went dark; an angry scowl contorted his features. He set her down and cuffed her soundly across the face with his open palm. "By God, you git into that saddle before I beat the hell out of you!"

She whirled to run, and he struck her with his fist. The force of the blow sent her sprawling. Before she could regain her feet he was onto her. Panting, cursing in his anger, he slammed her across the saddle. "Now, you little wildcat, you stay there or I'll tie you good an' proper," he snarled, and swung himself up behind her.

She must have fainted then. The next thing she knew they were riding. She dared not look around. She kept her eyes straight front lest a movement on her part encourage him to talk or bring from him some new, more revolting order.

The country they were passing through was unfamiliar: a land of cedars, juniper and scrub oak. They were following the windings of a dry creek's rocky bottom. Tumbled hills lay all about, yucca-studded, thorny with the tortured arms of cholla.

The sun's hot shafts were lengthening, throwing longer, darker shadows; telling her that night was not very far away. The sweet dry tang of evergreens was in the air, and the smell of dust and sunburned grass. She wondered where this man was taking her, and new alarm coursed through her as she pictured a host of nameless terrors conjured by her inexperience. But in the end that very inexperience was her salvation; she had no basis for comparisons, no background of knowledge from which to view her plight. She only knew this man was taking her away from home, from the harsh contours of bleak spires and rugged bastions that had grown familiar, from Maverick Canyon which for as long as memory served had been the only home she knew. Perhaps, she thought, he was taking her to the Y Bench, to that great ranch that lay beyond the south horizon. It must be the Y Bench, she reasoned, and this man a Y Bench puncher; Paw could wax right eloquent when it came to Y Bench matters. Y Bench was the only enemy they had, she guessed; it was the only one Paw talked about. Seemed as if the Y Bench wanted their canyon for some reason, and old Cowles Proctor, who owned the outfit, always got the things he wanted. But he wouldn't get their canyon, by grab; Paw'd said he wouldn't.

She was victim to swift vagaries of thought; to complex and conflicting emotions, more than half of which she did not understand. She did not understand why this man was taking her away. What could the Y Bench want of her? Or was he taking her for himself? The thought was scarcely credible; yet here she was running off with him like any runaway hussy. Paw'd be mad as hops. He'd give her a tannin' sure when she got back. Or maybe she wasn't going back!

It was a pretty disquieting thought. She pondered it a long while, scowling, turning over its various aspects. Suppose—Hang it all, she'd ask him. Without turning round, she said: "Are you takin' me to the Y Bench, stranger?"

"The Y Bench? Haw!" he chuckled. "You're a cute one, you are. The Y Bench! Haw! I guess not—that bunch of sons never did Buck Fiori any favors! You shut up now an' ride quiet-like or I'll put a hobble on your jaw," he told her gruffly, and urged the horse to faster motion.

The man's strange speech roused all her fears afresh. She could not shake the dread of nameless peril. If not to the Y Bench, where was he taking her? There were a lot of hard monkeys in the hills, Paw said; mebbe this was one of them— some outlaw hiding out who wanted a woman round his place. She tried to think what it would be like, being an outlaw's woman. She guessed it wouldn't be much fun. Paw said they were a shiftless, schemin' lot—a bunch of no-accounts teamed up to steal what honest fellows worked for.

And there was something else contributing to her worries. A phrase of Paw's. If only she'd been a boy, he'd say, or hadn't been so handsome. She'd heard him say it a hundred times. But he'd never give any reason for it. He said it mostly after some happenchance drifting prospector had put up with them for the night. Lately, though, Paw hadn't been putting up any. "Let 'em ride on someplace else," he'd say. "Drop a bullet 'crost their saddlebow 'f they won't take a plain hint, dang 'em! I ain't runnin' no golrammed hotel!"

She guessed it was on account of his mine. Paw was so durn crotchety, though, a body couldn't tell. But she knew he worried a lot about it. Never would get the thing recorded, and always took his ore way the hell up to Hillsboro where he sent it out on the stage. "Man can't be too careful," he'd tell her darkly, and was always recounting tales about luckless prospectors, about fellows who'd had their claims jumped. It seemed as if there were hombres in this world who spent nigh all their time jumping people's claims. The world, she guessed, must be a wicked place—like Sodom and Gomorrah. She hoped this man wouldn't take her far.

Once she recalled her mother who'd cashed in and gone to Jesus when she was just a little shaver; and for a while a strange, sweet peace came over her.

But it didn't last. The reality was too vivid, the whispering terrors of her plight too close. The rubbing of the saddle chafed her, was constantly reminding her of the fearful dangers she was sure must lie ahead. She thought about them, brooded on them until a blur came across her vision. At last, unable longer to contain herself, forgetful of his orders, she blurted another question. "You—you ain't a-takin' me to Haigler, are you?"

She felt the quick, hard impact of his eyes. She did not need to look to know that he was scowling; the fierceness of his scrutiny bit into her like a thorn. For a while she thought he did not mean to answer, he took so long about it. When he did speak, it was to growl defiantly: "An' what if I am—eh? What about it?"

She almost swooned with shock. Haigler! The worst of her fears were realized. This man was taking her to Haigler! She shivered visibly, recalling too well the three times she had met him. That first time when he'd come to talk with Paw about some mining matter, his eyes had been forever sliding round to stare at her till, fidgety, she'd got up and gone outside. And that second time—that humiliating time he'd found her bathing in the pool; and that third time when, alone with him in the cave-house, she'd thrown the pitcher and in a fury had grabbed up her Sharps and told him: "Git!" She could still recall the frenzy of that moment; the wolflike glitter of Haigler's eyes, the feel of his arms, his quick, hot breath. She still could shudder at the way he'd wrestled round with her, striving to effect some evil purpose, till she'd broken loose and got her gun sights trained dead on him. She'd never found the courage to tell Paw about that business. She thought now of what this stranger, this Rush Rago, had said: "Not if his intentions is good ones." Well, she'd never imagined they had been!

And now this man was taking her to Haigler; he was *not* a Y Bench puncher—hadn't anything to do with Proctor's ranch. He was taking her to some secret place where Haigler sat gloating, waiting.

She was really afraid now—vividly. From the first moment Haigler'd seen her he had wanted her. She had read it in his glances, had known it that day in the cave-house; and ever since the knowledge had spread an abiding gloom across her thoughts. Had it not been for her unfortunate encounter with Haigler, she might not so have resented Rago's impetuous kiss. She could not be sure of this; but she was very certain she wanted nothing more to do with Haigler. The very thought of him filled her with a quaking dread. She had wakened one night in an ecstasy of terror, bathed in sweat, with the feel of his arms around her. A nightmare—but it had left her depressed and shuddering for days.

She was agonized at the thought of how this ride was bound to end in another contact with the man—perhaps a final one. Suddenly sick and dizzy, she swayed dangerously in the saddle; and might have fallen had not her captor, with a curse, caught hold of her. Drooping over the pommel, her eyes hard shut, she fought the nausea gripping her; fought to keep her head, to sustain the shock of this paralyzing knowledge. Far from understanding it, she glimpsed now something of the really appalling nature of her plight. Glimpsed enough to guess what this compulsory visit to Haigler must hold in store.

That he dared use force to bend her to his will astounded her. She had not dreamed that men could be like that. Living most of her life with Paw in their lonely, isolated canyon, she'd been too sheltered, too out of contact with the world to guess that such things happened. She'd believed that folks who read their Bibles and minded their own business were left alone. She'd known, of course, that badmen roved the hills, held up stages and plundered ranches. But that any man dared steal a woman in this country—it was incredible.

Yet it was true.

She had told this man she did not want to go with him, had made it very plain. Yet she was with him, overcome by force, compelled to do his bidding. The reality of it was astounding— made her senses reel.

Yet it was the significance of her capture, the unmentionable purpose of it, that finally acted as a spur to Clementine's raw courage. While she lived there was hope; there was a chance of retaliation. She might yet, if she used her wits, come out on top. She must please this man, must obey his every order, foreguess his every wish. His suspicions must be lulled, his vigilance made to seem foolish until such time as she could turn the tables.

He would have his weaknesses; she must find them, take them into grim account.

Summoning all her will-power, steeling herself, she twisted in the saddle, turned and looked at him. Of average size, with no peculiarities of build, he wore a dark blue vest picked out with silver buttons, batwing chaps that were new and flashy with their whang strings and gleaming conchas, brass-studded, hand-tooled·leather cuffs and fancy Hyer boots. His belt and scabbard were of well-oiled, pliable leather, black like his chaps and cuffs. A snakeskin band encircled his tall San An hat.

He smiled as he took in her inspection, rasped a hand across his jaw and finally grinned. "No sense you tryin' to remember me. I ain't important. Besides, like enough you ain't goin' back where memory'll be doin' you any good," he grunted shrewdly.

She managed a faint laugh. "Goin' back? Good Lord, I hope not. I'm plumb glad to get away."

"Yeah. You acted like it," he said drily.

"That was when I didn't know what-all you was up to. Different now. Goin' to see Phil Haigler suits me powerful well. I'd begun to think he'd forgot plumb all about me," she said, flushing.

"You'd be a hard one to forget."

She fidgeted under his scrutiny. The bold light in his glance made her cheeks feel as hot as fire, and she had all she could do to control an impulse to spring from the saddle. "I guess you're funnin' me," she said faintly. She guessed she was acting like a fool, but it was the best that she could do. If he knew the way her heart was pounding . . .

He said with sudden eagerness: "What say we chuck this an' go off some place on our own?"

The vibrant timbre of his voice, the tightened pressure of his arm, pulsed new fear through

101

her arteries. She could not control the shudder that ran through her; resurgence of her terror threatened to overwhelm her utterly. But in the nick of time, shocked to caution by the bright intensity of his glance, she said: "I guess you don't savvy Phil much, do you? Why, he'd foller us from hell to breakfast! He ain't no man to cross like that. I—" she gave him a nervous smile—"I wouldn't dass to—honest."

Some of the hardness left his eyes, but the scowl still rode his features. The horse carried them several strides before he spoke. Relaxed a little, he then said sullenly: "Some squirts have all the luck, by God."

But she had her cue; without understanding it, she sensed the vanity of his nature. " 'F it wa'n't for Phil," she said, playing up to it, "I'd go off with you sure. You're my idea of what a man should be—my kind of hombre, mister. But Phil—" she didn't have to try to shiver—"he'd sure fetch me a right good tannin' if I tried it. An' he'd gun you, sure as hell."

He grunted something sultry about a Colt making all men equal, but she could see that he was flattered. His hold grew a little more comfortable; less rough, less alertly vigilant. She said: "Whereabouts do you cal'late that we'll be findin' him?"

The man straightened bony shoulders and gave her an intent, narrow stare. "Don't let it fret you none. Reckon you'll know when we get there."

She knew by the way he said it he hadn't much liked that question. She would have to be more careful. To arouse suspicion now would be to ruin all—to cancel the last slim chance. Her job was to play up to him. She must keep him flattered, for vanity was this man's chief weakness; eyes and clothes both said so, and there was a pride in his ways as well. A pride, she guessed, that would impel him into running risks no other could be hired to take; things smarter men would laugh to scorn—such as this risk he was piling up now. If he were caught with her it would be *his* neck—not Phil Haigler's—that would grace a hangman's hemp.

They had entered another canyon now, traveling a dim-seen trail beneath high yellow walls. She guessed it was getting sunset time above because, occasionally, looking upward, she glimpsed great crags along the rim glowing bright as gold against the far-away turquoise sky. Down here the evening gloom was thickening into twilight, casting shaggy yucca and multi-armed cholla into distorted, fearsome shapes. Time and again the crashing of some animal into the hemming chaparral attested to the region's wildness.

They made no stops. Out of one canyon and into another; on and on and on. The trail grew steeper and the light less useful, and Clementine became conscious of an aroused hunger while the aspect of the land grew steadily more unwelcome. Quail thrummed, rabbits scuttled, and once an elk lumbered out of the shadows with such suddenness that she guessed by the gruffness of the fellow's muttered curse he'd almost shot it for a rider.

The man seemed to know his way. At places where the trail forked or side canyons opened up he never hesitated, never slowed or gave any sign of being the least in doubt. She wondered how he knew these backland trails so well. He was not a mountain man.

She tried thinking up some strategy with which she might beguile the fellow, but none of the things that came to mind seemed anywhere near good enough. She must not chance any slip. Once on his guard, the man would countenance no second trick.

The trail had been climbing upward; the canyon walls had dwindled. Ahead lay a long and shallow valley almost level as a plain. Off in yonder distance dark mountain peaks leaned back against the sky, strange and somber, affording no marks that she could recognize. It was a wild and wondrous place, with grasses belly-deep to a horse, shaded by willow and spruce and hemlock, cut by a tiny stream whose purling waters struck a note of peace in the girl's troubled mind.

For some purpose best served by silence, her captor had stopped their horse and was peering round. The cut of his shoulders was queerly tense, and the eyes that quartered surrounding coverts were narrowed, intent, suspicious.

"What is this place?"

"Lost Valley—we're in the Little Burros," he said gruffly. "Now keep still. There's somethin' damn—"

He broke off with a curse, wheeling round with a hand flatting hipward as an abruptly stifled nicker came from a stand of willow two hundred yards to the left.

This was her chance!

Clementine grabbed wildly for the hand clamping round his gun-butt.

A quiet voice spoke from an edge of spruce twenty feet to the right.

"That's all right, ma'am. Just let him draw it."

Chapter 12

"REMEMBER—"

Rush looked at Paw and grunted. He said: "I've seen some pretty ornery roosters in my time, but—"

"Stow the gab," Paw growled, "an' get at it."

Rush was minded for a minute to fold his arms and tell the old fool where to go to. Nothing riled him like being prodded; but the girl's need finally won and he struck off, rifle in hand, head bent, eyes searching sign of the departed horse.

Half an hour took them out of the canyon and into another that was equally dry. Paw said this was Willow Creek's course and that the girl's abductor was probably making for the water that was in flow farther down. When they came to it Paw was proved right. The tracks went into the water and, though Paw took one bank and Rush the other, they followed the stream for twenty minutes without seeing the tracks come out.

"Back an' cut fer sign," Paw growled, but Rush shook his head. "Still in the water," he said, and pointed out a hoof-scratched rock. "Waitin' for a side canyon."

One presently opened, and Paw said sneeringly: "Here it is. Now where's your sign?"

Rush pointed. "See that rock? They came out there."

But Paw saw nothing on the rock to indicate the fact. "We'll stay with the stream a spell."

"Stay if you like."

Paw said: "You'll find that gal if you know what's good fer you."

"Look there. See that grass?"

"What about it?"

"Don't you see that broken twig? See that other one standin' up? It ain't growin' that way. You can go to hell if you want to, but *I'm* goin' up this gulch."

And he started off.

With a smothered oath Paw swung in behind him, eyes roving the crumbled rim, hand swinging close to his pistol.

They went a long way without further talk. Several times the old man must have caught glimpses of the track Rush followed, for he muttered darkly to himself and kept scowling up at the crack of sky above them and urging Rush to greater speed.

They left the canyon presently and entered another. With a loud exhalation of breath, Rush stopped and mopped the sweat from his face and neck. "Trail goes off down there." He pointed. "You know this country. Got any idea where they're headed for?"

"You're doin' all right. Get goin'."

107

"You want to come up with 'em, don't you? It's goin' to be dark in another couple hours. After that you'll read no sign till morning. None o' my business, of course, but was Clementine kin of mine—"

He quit on that note and looked at the old man slanchways. Paw met the look with a scowl and stared off down the canyon. Rush picked up a stick and made some marks in the sand. Hunkered on his boot heels, he said: "That's the way we've come up to now. This here," he said, adding another line, "represents that canyon you been peerin' down. I don't know much about this country, but I should think you might figure where they're goin' from this. Without knowing anything about it, just from readin' sign, I'd say they was cuttin' east. Anything likely over that way?"

Paw said: "You're mighty damn good at this sign readin'. 'Bout the best I ever seen. 'Dyou plan this layout for 'em?"

"Plan hell!" Rush said, and snorted. "What the hell'd I ever do to earn that kinda lingo? Quit actin' like a bad tooth an' show a little natural worry about your daughter. Whoever's grabbed her ain't takin' her to no picnic."

The old man's sourness thickened. He said through skinned-back lips: "Never mind all that—it's my concern. What I wanta know is what you been, where you been, an' what you're doin' usin' my place for a hideout. Suppose you habla on that a spell." There was heady menace in the brightness of his gaze.

Nor did Rush miss it. But he was not the sort to trim his sails. He'd no idea what he'd been or where he'd been; his memory was still vacationing. But he knew damn well he wasn't using this old hombre's place for any hideout. He told him so without choosing his language. He said: "If you've a spark of love for that girl of yours, quit jawin' an' put your mind to figurin' where they're headin' for. Course they *might* have grabbed her for a ransom, but—"

"What give you that idee?"

There was a sharpened edge to Paw's quick words. His body was canted forward now, and the fixity of his frozen interest gave him a definite, dangerous look.

But Rush, still squatted on his boot heels, sent the man a cool, wry grin. "The stuff you got in them gunnysacks," he drawled, and watched a change of expression grab the old man's cheeks and twist them, watched the muscles working in his shoulders and the patent strain that was clawing its way across the dark, seamed features.

The next moment he was staring down the barrel of Paw's big pistol, bracing himself for the explosion, cold waves washing up his spine.

"So you been pryin' into them, too, hev you?"

The jerk of that bony shoulder was something

Rush had expected—waited for. He came surging up from his boot heels, hurling himself against the gnarled old frame, caroming into it—reaching out and snapping a hold on the old man's lifting hand.

The gun went off. Rush felt the burst of powder, the jarring blast of driven air. Then he was shoving his knee hard against Paw's belly, and with a quick twist had got possession of the heavy gun. Paw rocked back against a sapling; swayed there, fighting for breath and cursing all in one. Rush doubled a fist and said: "You willin' to call it quits now?"

"No!" snarled Paw malignantly. "You brash young fool, I'll—"

Rush shook his head. "I guess not. Leastways not right now. Right now we're goin' to hunt your daughter." He tucked the old man's pistol in his belt and tossed him over the rifle. "A six-gun's more my style," he said. "Now get this straight: I don't give a damn if you got forty mines—not if each one's worth a million. I ain't a minin' man—"

"That ain't what you told Clem," Paw growled. "Told her you was a burro man—was up here huntin' gold!"

Rush said, astonished: "Did I? That's queer, ain't it? Don't remember it at all. Fact is, I never was a minin' man—don't know a thing about it."

"You ain't tellin' me! I spotted you right off, first lick I saw you. You're a goddam sneakin' range dick! That's what you are!"

Rush stared, astounded. Then he slowly shook his head. "I'm afraid, ol' man, you're barkin' at the wrong persimmon—but we'll settle all that stuff later," he said with a growled impatience. "Thing now is to find your daughter. Whereabouts d'you figure they're headin' for? Any chance of cuttin' them off? Any short cuts we can shank to?"

The old man took a deep breath. With his cheeks still raw, his bright glance sulky, he grunted: "That yonder's Red Rock Canyon. Swings north a spell here but bends south after a piece; hits down towards that new place they call Tyrone—headquarters of the Burro Mountain Copper crowd. 'Tween here an' there's a hell's own devil of a country, all cut to hell an' gone with gulches, canyons, 'royos an' what not." He glared at Rush defiantly. "Be like huntin' fer a needle in a haystack."

"Good hideout country, sounds like. Man can get through, can't he? Any special place you'd pick if you was doin' it?"

Paw growled: "Lost Valley—" and then, real quick-like, locked his face up tight in a scowl that was bitterly hostile.

Rush affected not to see. He said: "Lost Valley," musingly. Then: "Ain't that a rustler's hangout?"

"I don't know a goddam thing about it," Paw said sullenly.

"We'll find out somethin' then," Rush said. "Reckon you could get there, couldn't you? There's a short cut a man on foot could use, I reckon, ain't there?"

The old man scowled and hesitated, seeming to weigh something in his mind. That secret thinking laid its mark on his bristly features and somehow, unaccountably sent a prickly chill across the back of Rush's bent neck. He wondered what new trick the old fool had up his sleeve; but didn't wonder long. For suddenly, with a brief, jerky nod, Paw trotted off, rifle slung in the hollow of an arm, long strides propelling him out of the canyon, breaking a new, hard trail south by east.

Up and down Rush followed, quartering the tumbled hills. The going was rough, the pitches stiff, and sweat came out and drenched his shirt, coating it with a white salt brine. The smash of sun flayed across their backs; every stone of those rock-littered slopes seemed to hold its quota of refracted heat; the hillsides pulsed with it and the snaky arms of ocatilla appeared to float in its visible shimmer.

Forgotten country, Rush thought, mopping the smarting wetness off his face—forgotten alike by God and man; left by the Indians, the abode of the lizard, the horned toad and sidewinder. The sparse curled grass was scorched and withered, even the rocks were black and blistered, and the sun poured down like melted copper, baking the earth to a red-rust brown made leprous by great patches of chalky orange that stood bare as a beggar's sores.

A country shot by the lean, stiff shafts of yucca, spiked with cholla and Spanish bayonet, cut and cracked and gutted. The only moisture in the whole damn land was the sweat the sun boiled out of them. There was no shade save the hand's-breath shadow cast by stunted juniper; no color but the corrosive mauve and rust.

On and on and on. Floundering, stumbling, in some places crawling, the trip would have done a Penitent proud. But Rush was not of that order; he had to grit his teeth and put a will-clamped hobble on his jaw to keep from showing the strain. He felt like a man in a nightmare.

He looked up suddenly to find Paw stopped. The old man stood with shoulders slanted, peering through the twilit trees. "Your valley's yonder. See 'em any place?"

Rush looked. Leaning his weight against a scrub oak's roughening bark, he dragged a sleeve across his burning eyes. Again he studied what lay visible of that broad expanse before them. "No," he said, finally shaking his head. "Prob'ly haven't got here yet—"

"*If* they're comin'," the old man said unchar-itably.

Rush turned somber eyes on him. "If they ain't, you better start roundin' up what prayers you know. That girl of yours'll sure be needin' 'em." He looked once more across the darkening distance. "Which way does that trail cut into this place?"

Paw jerked his head. "Over there. Bit more to your left. There's forty places, though," he muttered, "where they coulda left it—coulda cut fer other parts. What I say is that we'd ort to follered the sign."

Rush didn't bother with that one. He said: "Got any shells for that Sharps you're totin'?"

"Ort to be three-four cartridges in it."

"Ever hear what 'ort' did to the Mexican?"

Paw growled: " 'F you'd spend as much of your time mindin' your own business as you do dreamin' up them damn fool saws, you might amount—"

"I amount to plenty right now, old man, so far as you're concerned," Rush scowled. "Hadn't been for me you'd still be running circles back in that canyon. You may savvy how to hunt a mine, but—"

He left off, putting a hard look on the man's changed face as Paw half lifted the rifle. "Go ahead," he challenged. "Go ahead an' try that on if you want to get your ears batted down to where they'll do for wings. I ain't beholden to you nohow. 'F it had been left to you, I reckon

I'd been down some buzzard's gullet an' out again by now. More I see of you the better I like sidewinders."

Paw didn't like that talk by a little bit, but he lowered the rifle. Rush's tough face flagged a warning; there was that about him which hinted that he was no safe man to monkey with, and Paw had been around enough to know it.

But if Paw sensed the hard efficiency of Rush's young nature, Rago for his part was well aware of the old man's dangerousness. This old pelican, enraged by Rush's acquired knowledge of those found gunnysacks, would not scruple to put him out of the way if opportunity presented. Every vestige of the man's deportment, every covert look from those smouldering eyes bespoke the hatred that was gnawing him. Suspicion was as much a part of Paw as the earth-stained clothes he wore, and Rush's brash mention of the gunny-sacks had fanned that flame to fever heat. Continued health, Rush realized, would depend on how much care and vigilance he was capable of.

But he was not the man to be distracted from the issue. He might not care to marry Clementine—was not, in fact, the least bit anxious to get hooked up with any skirt—but he was not unappreciative of her kindness. She had nursed him through a damn bad gunshot wound, had very likely saved his life, and the chance was here to repay her.

He said: "Hike over an' cache yourself in that brush off there to the left. If they come this way an' the guns start poppin', get into it. An' be goddam careful where you throw your lead. If things go quiet, leave the play to me."

The old man stared at him morosely. "You wouldn't be lettin' the damn' hound go . . . ?"

Rush said irritably: "How can I tell what I'll do? Leave it that way till I see the fellow—till I hear what he's got to say."

"He'll not pull no damn freight while I'm fixed handy with a rifle!"

Rush eyed him silently, grimly. He said at last: "Where's that canyon empty out?"

"That dark gash over there between them hogbacks." Paw said doggedly: "Remember—I'll not see the son git away." He wheeled abruptly, shambling off in the curdled gloom.

Rush stood and watched him go and with a muttered oath hunkered down against his tree. He drew the pistol from his belt and felt it over point by point with practiced hands. Grunting softly, he laid it handy on the ground beside him and folded his arms across his knees and brooded on the curse of his lost identity, wondering bitterly who he was and why he'd come to such desolate country. He wondered mostly how he'd come to throw his lot with such a man as Paw, and what Paw had been before he had built that crazy cave-house; and how it was that Paw's girl possessed such wild-rose beauty, such challenging eyes, such bewitching ways; and what—if anything—might lie between herself and him.

He sat a long time with his thoughts. The moon came up, smoothing away the harshness of this country's contour, filling the distance with an argent splendor. Once he thought he heard the muffled clumps of nearing hoofbeats and then, much later, moonlight showed a drift of dust along the canyon's edge and a tired horse's clatter hushed the night life round him.

Chapter 13

THE MARSHAL THINKS

It was close to four in the morning when a low, insistent tapping roused Durango from his sleep. He swung his legs from the cot, as awake on the instant as a banker shaved and breakfasted, and quietly, barefooted, gun in hand, he moved to the jail's glass-fronted door. He stood for a moment in the gloom beside it, inspecting the knocker with the caution of a man who had not always ridden the right side of the law's tall fence. Then, with a muttered oath, thankful none of the cells held occupants, he admitted his visitor and carefully fastened the door behind him.

He eyed the man with disfavor. "I told you, Bransen—"

"I know what you told me. You said if Haigler left town to foller him. He left, an' I did, an' I got a lot to tell you—too damn much to put in any note! Got a drink? I'm drier'n a frog in Arizona, an' this is goin' to take a little time."

The marshal eyed him a moment longer, then led the way to his living quarters at the back. Carefully lowering the shades, he lit a lamp; produced bottle and glasses from a cupboard and, putting them on a table, indicated a chair.

118

Bransen was a big man—even for that country where big men were the rule. A hulking mountain of a man, he waddled to the table, swigged his liquor from the bottle and seated himself with a grunt that made the chair creak. The dirt-lined cracks of his triple-chinned face were twisted with excitement—an excitement plain enough to rouse the marshal's impatience.

"Come on," he growled. "Get busy an' spill it."

Bransen eyed him with a grin. "You sure had the right tip when you said to foller Haigler. That guy's a catamount fer nerve! He—"

"Will you tell it or—"

"All right, all right; take it easy. Rome wasn't built in no day. 'Bout four-fifteen yesterday afternoon this Haigler sport went down to the livery, got a horse an' went sashayin' off up Fortuna Canyon. I thought, first off, I was headed on a wild goose chase, because he stopped off at one of them 'dobe houses fer a spell chinnin' with some gal. I could see him talkin' with her on the porch—good looker, too, an'—Aw right! I'm gettin' there."

He reached for the bottle, but Durango moved it. "You can have the rest after I hear the story."

Bransen scowled, seemed about to protest, then with a shrug resumed his account. "After mebbe fifteen minutes he said goodbye to the dame, got on his horse an' kept on up the canyon. When he'd left town well behind, he cut a circle clean around it an' lines out northwest at a right smart canter. I gave him a pretty good start because, goin' that way, there's a lot of hills an' hogbacks an' I didn't want him lookin' back an' seein' me. Fella like that, you can't never tell.

"Well, I let him get ahead a piece an' kep' my eye on the sign—not all the time, though, mind you. I kep' one eye cocked fer trouble. An' lucky I did, too! 'Bout five-six miles out this catamount pulls up—see? Just in case, I reckon. He'd slowed up right consider'ble. 'Cause all of a sudden I happens t' look off to the right, an' by Gawd there he was, pullin' over behind a alder thicket—"

"See you?"

"No. But I sure piled off that nag in a hurry! Clapped a hand across his whistle an' backed him into some handy oak. An' jest in time. Squintin' through the branches that way, I could see this Haigler rakin' the backtrail with a pair of glasses. Made a good thorough job of it, too. I thought fer a while he'd lamped me, he looked so damn hard at my oak patch. But after a coupla minutes he put his glasses up an' started m'anderin' off again.

"I let him go. I give him ten minutes, not wantin' no more of that stuff with mebbe me pilin' into a bullet. Wasn't no rush; he was takin' it pretty easy now. Where the hell d'you reckon he was goin'?"

Durango shook his head.

"Well, give a guess."

"Hell's fire! 'Swhat I'm payin' you good money to come an' tell me," growled the marshal, in a sweat at the fellow's protractions.

"Well," said Bransen, "he was goin' up in the Little Burros—to no less a place'n Lost Valley!" he declared, banging his fist down on the table.

"Lost Valley, eh?" Durango looked very thoughtful. Then he glanced up with a scowl. "What about it? Get on with it. You ain't goin' to tell me that's where the trail run out—?"

"Run out nothin'!" Bransen grinned. "I follered him right on in. I wasn't over a hundred yards off when the fireworks started. You sh'd of seen the look on his fancy mug when he found out somebody'd got in there ahead of 'im! I—"

"For cripes' sake tell the thing in order!" Durango snarled at him. "How the hell can I make out what you're gettin' at when you skip all—"

"O.K.—O.K. Remember you got high blood pressure—Well, I follered him into Lost Valley; I had 'im in sight when he went in there, so I was able to slip up pretty close to him without 'im gettin' wise. He seemed to be waitin' round for someone. Got off his bronc an' pulled its gear off; even hitched him to a picket pin. That give me time to look over the place a little. It was gettin' pretty dark about then; not dark, but gettin' that way. Haigler kep' lookin' over towards that pass that cuts down from Red Rock, so I took a squint over that way, too.

"Pretty soon I lamped a fella off to the left a ways sittin' with his back ag'in' a tree. I was lookin' from a different angle than this Haigler an', thinks I, betcha that's the bird he's lallin' round fer. But I was wrong, as you'll see direckly.

"All of us kep' waitin' like a bunch of buzzards fer a cow in a bog hole. After a spell the moon come up; made things kinda blue an' hazy an' I couldn't see this other gent so well. Couldn't see Haigler so damn good, either, so I starts workin' in closer. Took me best part of twenty minutes, but I got within twelve feet of 'im—"

"Will you stick to the point?" growled Durango. "I ain't interested in these details—I wanta know what happened."

"Well, after a bit," said Bransen, scowling, "I hears the sound of horse hoofs off towards the pass. An' pretty soon up pops a horse packin' double. Fella sittin' back of the saddle seemed to be runnin' things. He stops the nag right there in the trail an' sets kinda forward like he didn't much like the look of the place. He starts t' mutter somethin' to the other fella, an' right then Haigler's bronc lets out a whinny.

"Lord! You talk about hell with a chunk under it! Everythin' happens to oncet. Front rider grabs fer back rider's gun, Haigler grabs his bronc's whistler, an' that fella I'd seen settin' with his back to a tree says: 'That's all right, ma'am. Jest let 'im draw it'!"

"Ma'am?"

"*Ma'am!* That's what he said," grinned Bransen. "You coulda knocked me over with a wheat shuck. Bronc's front rider was that li'l wildcat from Maverick Canyon—what d'you thinka that?"

"What happened?" demanded Durango, leaning forward.

"Hell broke loose right! While the girl was wrasslin' round tryin' to get that fella's gun an' him tryin' to keep her from it, this pelican what had been cached out by the tree romps up an' planks his artillery in a front-line position. 'Git your hands up an' git down off that horse,' he says like he meant business. The guy does so, an' I might's well tell you now it was that wind-jammin' Buck Fiori. Never'da guessed he had the guts to cut a shine like that, but there he was an' there was the girl—"

"Did Haigler—?"

"Haigler never winked his blinkers. He kep' right still an' hung onto his horse's trumpet till you'd thought he growed there regular. Well, Fiori gets outa the saddle, an' this guy says: 'Just where was you aimin' to go to?' An' Buck says: 'None o' your damn so-an'-so!' An' the guy says—"

"What guy?"

"The guy what had been parkin' his fanny ag'in' the tree. *I* dunno who he is—never saw him round these parts. Some stranger, I reckon—but the girl, she knew him all right. She says: 'Rush!' all tight an' twitterin' like she'd never expect he'd get there. Anyway, this fella says to Fiori: 'I guess you know what happens to guys caught runnin' off women,' an' Fiori growls 'I wasn't runnin' off no woman—ask her,' an' this guy does. The girl says: 'He was takin' me to Haigler—' An' right there's where Fiori an' me an' ever'body else sure got one whale of a shock! Off to the left a ways a gun goes WHAM! an' Fiori folds up like a last year's leaf! He didn't even wiggle!"

"Who shot him?"

"Lubbock—that crack-pot coffee-cooler what's been prospectin' Maverick Canyon—"

"The girl's old man?" exclaimed Durango excitedly.

"Well, if he says so it's all right with me. I don't want no truck with that guy!" Bransen's tone was fervent.

"What happened then?"

"This Lubbock comes outa the brush with a Sharps an' the Rush fella starts to give him some jaw an' he puts the gun right on him. 'Git!' he says plumb ornery. 'An' git in a goddam hurry!' The Rush fella sticks his jaw out an' looks like he's figgerin' to make some further habla, but the girl says somethin' to him real quick an' he kinda hesitates like he ain't right sure what he is gonna do; an' Lubbock starts wavin' around his rifle. Finally the fella climbs up on Fiori's bronc. He says somethin' to the girl, an' she points this way, towards town. I coulda reached out an' touched him when he passed. The—"

"What did Lubbock do then?"

"Him an' the girl struck off across the hills—"

"And Haigler—"

"Haigler never said 'boo' the whole damn time. He'd guts enough to hatch the business up, but he wasn't wantin' any of Lubbock's medicine. Me, neither. I always say let well enough a—"

"Did you pull your freight?"

"I never pulled it better. How about unfreezin' yourself from that bottle fer a spell? All this gassin's hard on a man that's been doin' all the ridin' I been."

"Where's Haigler?"

"On 'is way back, I reckon—if he ain't already got here. Looks like he was figgerin' to grab the girl, don't it? Reckon he was playin' for a ransom?"

"What he was playin' for needn't concern you," said Durango shortly. "Here's some money; there'll be more when you report again. While you're keepin' tabs on Haigler, keep an eye skinned out for that stranger. If he hits town, I want to know it. Yes—yes, take the bottle with you, but see you keep your mouth shut. This business is under your hat. Just between the two of us."

Bransen nodded and, with the bottle firmly tucked beneath an arm, departed. The marshal sat with the light out, thinking.

Chapter 14

"COME SEE ME IN THE MORNING."

Ruddabaugh knew the moment he saw Bronc Forney that the man was ripe for mischief. The Y Bench super brought a piece of the night in with him, but it was not air-chilled enough to unlock those tight-warped cheeks from their pattern of sultry anger. Never had the fellow's eyes been as brash as this or his look so reckless. He was in a proper rage, and, knowing something of his irascible temper, the tavern-boss waited with interest.

"An' what'll it be this evenin', Bronc? Old Crow or a glass or two of Scotch?"

The Y Bench man ripped out a bitter curse. His slammed fist hit the bar with a force that made the bottles jump. The barman showed a gambler's face, but Ruddabaugh displayed concern. "What's up?" he said. "More cows run off or—"

Forney rasped a gusty oath. "I been sold down the river, that's what! Any fool that'll pardner coyotes an' jackals oughtn't expect no better. But by God, I *did* think Cowles was one man a fella could tie to! Turned me out like a worthless bum! Me that's put in the best years of my life makin' that place a ranch for him! Said: 'Get your check at the office, Forney; I want you off this spread by sundown. Get off an' don't come back!' "

He put down the drink the barman handed him like a dry man drinking water. He wiped his mouth with the back of a hand and put his bloodshot eyes on Ruddabaugh. "Think of it, Kurt—turned off the place like a goddam beggin' saddle tramp!"

Kurt Ruddabaugh shook his head. Putting his hands on the arms of his wheel chair, he leaned forward, regarding Forney curiously. "Don't seem possible. Why, Bronc? Why?" he murmured. "Whatever's come over Proctor? Don't he know—?"

"That's what I asked him. He says: 'Karvel can attend to things quite satisfactory. You're not any institution, Bronc; this place'll get along without you.' " The discharged super swore with malevolence. "No man can do that way with me. Mark my words, he'll—"

The sound of a phone bit through his talk with a loud, shrill clangor. Ruddabaugh wheeled himself across to the wall with a quiet apology, lifted the receiver from its special hook and pulled the hose affixed to the mouthpiece to a position where he could use it.

Forney, still glowering, watched him. Ruddabaugh's look gave nothing of his news away; his words held no clue to the caller's identity. His mouth flattened once as he listened. He said "yes" twice and when he was finished hung up.

He wheeled himself back to Forney. "Go ahead, Bronc."

"Ain't no ahead to it," Forney growled. "But there's sure as hell goin' to be a hereafter for a couple of hombres. An' that damn Karvel's one of 'em! I picked that hombre off the grub line, give him a foreman's job, an' this is what I get for it."

"Should think it would be Proctor you'd have your mad on at."

"Oh, I'll tend to him," muttered Forney. "I ain't forgettin' the years I put in makin' the Y Bench what it is; what a man can build he can pull down after him. The ones I'm after is . . ." He broke off with a belated caution, and sent a restless stare about the place. The only customers at the moment were two Mexicans from No. 1 Mine, but he said on a sudden thought: "Anyone usin' that back room, Kurt?"

Ruddabaugh shook his head.

"Let's go back there," Forney muttered, and the tavern boss signalled the barman to bring drinks.

"It's that sneakin' Karvel that I'm after mostly," Forney said when seated comfortably in the back room's privacy with a new-opened bottle at his elbow. "It's him talked me out of that job." He looked at Ruddabaugh cunningly. "Ever hear of a bird named Lubbock? . . . Coffee-cooler—filed on Maverick Canyon; two-by-four gulch up in the Burros."

Ruddabaugh inclined his head noncommittally. "Lots of prospectors doin' that nowadays. Seems to be a fever with 'em since the Company bought out the Leopold mine and paid hard cash for that fella's hole up in the canyon. Mostly what's got these birds to filing, though, is the trouble the Tiffany crowd had with the turquois diggings— clouded titles an' stuff like that. Always some chance of claim-jumping or the question of ownership cropping up. All these burro men are playin' safe now; they're filin' on, recording an' proving up everything they take a fancy to."

Forney waved all that aside. "The point is that this Lubbock's filed Maverick Canyon an' Cowles Proctor wants the place." His hard bright eyes watched the tavern man expectantly. "He's got a daffy notion that lost river goes under it some place an' wants to sink a few wells to find out. He's got the alfalfa bug now, you know, an' figures if he can get that river an' turn it down some top-of-the-ground channel he's got in mind, he can water a whole smear of range that ain't worth a whoop fer farmin' the way it stands."

"Well, that seems sensible," said Ruddabaugh cautiously. "Why don't he buy this Lubbock out?"

"The fool won't sell. Proctor offered fifty

thousand, an' he turned it down like money growed on trees. He hates Y Bench worse'n poison, somehow. Guess it's really Y Bench's size he hates; got some notion Proctor aims to cover the earth or somethin'. I dunno; but anyway Proctor asked me to find some way around him, an' I told him there wasn't any way. He sends for Karvel an' puts it up to him—"

"I expect Karvel suggested violence," said Ruddabaugh, expecting nothing of the sort.

"No. He said there was one sure way of gettin' the place—understand, I wasn't present when Karvel's masterpiece was discussed. But I heard about it!" The turmoil of his badgered, reckless soul spilled out. "Gosh knows I ain't no saint. I never put up to be! But I wouldn't sell my friends like a lousy three-ball usurer! That's what that damn Karvel did!"

Ruddabaugh said thoughtfully: "You mean he was friends with this desert rat, Lubbock?"

Forney's hand clenched the bottle irritably, the rage in him spilling the liquor as he poured. "He doesn't know Lubbock from Adam. He was in a deal with me an' that stiff-necked Haigler; it was us he sold, goddam him—an' did me out of my job!"

The eyes regarding Ruddabaugh held murder. This man, if the chance presented itself, and maybe if it didn't, would drop Karvel without a qualm. Would kill him as if he would a snake, or a dog that snapped at his heels. Bronc Forney in a mood like this was dynamite.

The tavern man nodded. "It's a long lane that has no turning," he offered carefully.

"This one's goin' to have a turnin' quick, by God—or I'll know the reason why. I'm goin' to put you next to somethin', Kurt. I'm goin' to tell you somethin' on'y three of us knows, an' I'm goin' to make you a proposition. Somethin' that'll beat peddlin' whiskey to these oilers hell-to-breakfast."

Ruddabaugh shrugged. "I'm makin' out all right."

"You can do a damn' sight better!" Forney's glance stabbed the room's one window; he got up and drew the shade. On soundless feet he crossed to the door, abruptly jerking it open. No one showed outside; nothing showed but night's cold black. Forney swung, crossing to the door giving onto the bar. He listened a moment, grunted, came back and dropped in his chair. "Grin if you like. There's a lot of squirts would give their pants to know what I'm goin' to tell you."

His searching glance was quick, intent. "Lubbock's struck gold—what I mean, he's struck it right. This ain't no piddlin' pocket. I've seen the stuff. Not samples—sacks. Picture rock—the kind you see in these brokers' winders. No float, mind you; this stuff's in place. I been there. So's Karvel—we was there together—

stumbled in one time when the ol' man an' the girl was off some place. Got a shack-house built in a cliff; the mine's in a cavern back of it."

"This what you an' Karvel an' Haigler been chinnin' so much about of late?"

Forney nodded. "I oughta known better'n to do any business with that Haigler; but I *did* expect a little better treatment outa Karvel." His raw, tough face was ugly, indescribably bitter. "It's things like this that tell you who your friends are. The three of us made a deal to grab that mine. I guess a third share wasn't enough for a enterprisin' gent like Karvel. He saw his chance to play whole hog an' took it. Told Cowles Proctor he could get that canyon for him all right; might take a little time, though—month, mebbe—an' that he'd want a hundred thousand if he pulled it off. I was there up to that point. Proctor hit the rafters; but I guess he come to it after I left. That was yesterday. This mornin' I got my walkin' papers."

Ruddabaugh could see how the memory galled him. He said: "What was this great plan?"

"Lubbock's got a daughter—wild young thing an' ignoranter'n Job's turkey. For a hundred thousand Karvel allows he'll marry this kid an'—case anything should happen to the ol' man meantime—turn the canyon water rights over to Proctor whenever he wants 'em."

The tavern boss whistled.

"Simple, eh?" Forney's grin was twisted.

"But why pay him a hundred thousand? I know plenty birds that would do it cheaper."

"Here, too—in fact, that's what Proctor told him. But Karvel's smart. He thought of the stunt, an' he got the Ol' Man's word in writin' before he spilled the plan. Somebody'll have to buy that damn ranny a new hat quick if he don't get what he's askin' for."

Forney scowled, poured more liquor into his glass and sat staring at it, brooding. Ruddabaugh, who'd played poker with the best, made no interruption. When Forney raised a red-rimmed glance to ask him what he thought of it, Ruddabaugh shrugged. "Let's hear your proposition first."

"You've heard it. I'm offerin' you a full half of Lubbock's mine."

The tavern boss grinned wryly. "Very nice, I'm sure. You know I'm tied to this chair. This in the nature of a donation for my friendly interest an' well-wishing?"

Bronc Forney scowled. "Not hardly—but I ain't askin' a powerful lot. All I want you to do is to see this Haigler keeps his jaw shut. I'm scourin' him off the slate. Won't have him fer a pardner—his tongue swings like a broken gate, an' way he acts you'd think he got orders t' boss this job from God Himself. You got a lot of Mex friends; oughta be a couple you can—"

"Well, I'll see. I'll have to think it over. I got some Mex friends—yes; but I don't know . . . I tell you, Bronc; I got a good thing here, a little slow maybe, but plenty sure. I don't know as I ought to risk it on a stunt like you got in mind. It's pretty brash and—"

"What the hell do you want? A picket fence around it?"

Ruddabaugh shrugged. "I want to sleep on it, anyway. It isn't I don't appreciate what you're wantin' to do for me, Bronc. It's just—well, it's not my kind of thing. An' there's a hell of a lot of people in the know."

"You call three fellas a lot?"

"Three's a lot in a deal like this. But there's more'n three knows about this mine. First of all there's Lubbock. Then there's you an' Haigler an' Karvel. There's me. There's Lubbock's daughter. That's six of us anyway. There may be more." He chewed his upper lip, frowning at the ex–Y Bench segundo. "Even admittin' Karvel's out-maneuverin' of you on that canyon-water angle, didn't it strike you there was something mighty queer about Proctor lettin' you go like that?"

Forney said: "I thought it goddam queer. But—"

"Like mebbe Karvel had dropped a few quiet tips . . . ?"

Forney's bony shoulders tensed. In that brash,

135

straw-colored stare the tavern boss could see all the old, balked rage of the man churning through his mind again. It was like rekindled flame licking through the black of stamped-out char. Then something checked it—some remembrance. Logic spread a film of oil across the tumult of the wild inferno Ruddabaugh had roused. He said reluctantly: "He'd never dare—he couldn't do it without somehow tyin' in himself, Kurt. He'll be wantin' Proctor's hundred grand too bad to try a stunt like that."

"He could get the hundred thousand still," Ruddabaugh murmured slowly. He regarded the rug spread across his lap with a far-off, contemplative look. "He might figure the hundred thousand a whole lot surer an' safer than any percentage he might wangle from the mine. At the same time he could clinch his value to Proctor—"

"What the hell you gettin' at?" Forney pulled himself up straight. He spoke with sudden savagery, the straw-colored eyes, ripe wheat in his brick-red face, gone abruptly violent. "If there's somethin' in your mind, come out with it—put it down where I can see it."

"Well, it strikes me Karvel's play was better than you figure." He let his breath out gently, saying carefully: "Nothing that you've told me would account for Proctor firin' a man who's been with him as long as you have. As I see it,

136

what Karvel did was this: He told Proctor he could get him his canyon by marrying Lubbock's daughter and, in case of an accident taking Lubbock off, he'd then be in a position where he could deed Y Bench those water rights. I believe he told Proctor then that he'd stumbled on something putting a different complexion on the matter; that'd he'd discovered that you, working hand and glove with Haigler, were interested in that canyon personally. That things seemed to indicate Lubbock had made some kind of strike he was keeping secret, and that you an' Haigler were out to do the old man in and jump it."

Forney stared at him incredulously. "Lord— he'd never cut his throat like that! Be givin' the whole damn show away! How could he expect—"

"Just the same," said Ruddabaugh grimly, "I'm bettin' that's what he did. Mebbe he's got better information on that strike than you have; mebbe the vein pinches out—"

"You're batty as hell!" cried Forney. "That ledge—"

"All right." The tavern boss waved a protesting hand. "I'll take your word for it. But there's a joker in this some place. I'll have to think it over. Tell you what, Bronc. Come see me in the morning an' I'll let you know where I stand."

Forney looked at him long and carefully. Finally he shook his head and rose. "You're a queer duck, Kurt—queerest duck I ever seen. A man dumps half a million in your lap an' you tell him you'll have to think it over. I can't make you out."

Ruddabaugh smiled drily. "Put it down to native caution if you want. I never like to jump till I know where I'm goin' to land. But I'll think on it. Come see me in the morning."

Chapter 15

TEN A.M.

The owner of the Wheel House Bar had just
wound up his breakfast when one of his gamblers
stepped in to say Durango wanted to see him.

"Durango, eh? What about?"

"He didn't mention. But by the look in his eye
I'd say you better see him."

"He in a hurry?"

"He didn't say so."

"What time is it, Kearney?"

"Goin' on towards ten."

"Well, tell him to come in."

The marshal came in on the balls of his feet. He
leaned against the wall, fishing the makings from
his pocket, and did not speak till the gambler
left the room and closed the door. He looked at
Ruddabaugh, watching him inscrutably while he
rolled his smoke.

Ruddabaugh said genially: "Had your breakfast
yet, Les? Toby's still got plenty on the stove in
case—"

"I didn't come here for a meal," Durango murmured. There was an undercurrent of vibrancy in
his steady, watching stare that would have made
a lesser man uneasy; a quiet kind of searching

139

scrutiny that betokened unusual interest. An official interest, a man might almost have said.

But Ruddabaugh seemed not to notice. "Looks like we might be going to get a little rain," he said. "The range can use it—"

"An' I didn't come to talk about range or cattle," Durango told him. He said enigmatically: "On the coast they got a term industrialists are usin' nowadays. You ought to look into it. Over-expansion. Seems to fit your case."

Ruddabaugh met that sloe-eyed stare with a ready chuckle. "Mean you think I'm doin' too well at this business?"

"I'm wonderin'. Bronc Forney was killed last night."

Ruddabaugh's face displayed the right surprise. "Where'd it happen?"

"Down at the Pines. He was stayin' at that dude ranch. Did you know old Proctor'd fired him?"

The tavern boss nodded. "As a matter of fact I did. He dropped in last night an' mentioned it."

The marshal's stare held an edge of disappointment. "What did you an' him find to chin about so long?"

Ruddabaugh shrugged. "It was Bronc did most of the chinnin'. He was pretty sore about the way he got let out. Seemed to have it in for Karvel more'n he did for Proctor—said Karvel had talked him out of his job. Mostly hot air, I reckon. He was hittin' the booze pretty hard." His eyes met Durango's curiously. "You say he was killed at Carter's?"

"I said he was killed at the Pines. He was staying at Carter's. As a matter of fact, his body was found at the ford. . . . One of the Mex maids come across him this morning."

Ruddabaugh said interestedly: "Found any clues to the business? Any idea who done him in?"

"I been thinkin'," Durango remarked with an elaborate casualness, "mebbe you might have somethin' to offer." It was a bright, searching look that he put on the man, but Ruddabaugh shook his head.

" 'Fraid not, Les. I don't get the news like I used to. Somethin' come over this camp. The Mexes have got that close-mouthed you'd think they was bein' paid for it."

"You were the last man," Durango said bluntly, "to see Bronc Forney alive."

The tavern boss leaned a bit forward in his chair to eye the marshal with a more careful regard. The look held speculation, and other things not so easily read. He said: "You're not suggesting . . . ?"

"I'm not suggestin' anything. I'm statin' a known fact, Ruddabaugh." Durango licked his cigarette, put it in his mouth and, with his eyes still watching the other's features, struck a match to it. "There were two oilers in your bar when

Forney was over here shootin' off his mouth. I've talked to both of 'em. What were you an' Forney talkin' about all that time in your back room?"

Ruddabaugh said patiently: "I've told you, Les. It was Bronc did all the talkin'. Just like out in the bar. He kep' swingin' his jaw about Karvel, an' how Karvel had done him out of his Y Bench job, an' how he was goin' to even the score if it took him the rest of his natural life and—Oh, yes! He wanted to know if I couldn't make him some kind of job here to sort of tide him over till he got on with another spread. But, hell, you know I couldn't use a man like Forney around this place—he's a sight too brash an' headlong. I told him to come round an' see me in the mornin'—"

Durango's shoulders stirred impatiently. "Didn't mention Haigler, did he?"

"I wondered if you'd ask me that. As a matter of fact, he did. Said something about the possibility of Haigler's getting him on with Crow-Rondack . . . some kind of a straw boss' job, seemed like. He—"

Durango growled: "Quit beatin' the goddam bushes! You know what I mean! Forney was in with Karvel an' Haigler on some kind of under-hand business—you know it well as I do. Sure he didn't say somethin' about them havin' a falling out? Somethin' that might account for him gettin' that one-way ticket?"

The marshal's slitted eyes were darkly searching. His cheeks were couched in suspicious lines. Ruddabaugh shook his head. Durango said: "Damn queer, him doin' all that gassin' an' never once bringin' up his connection with them two. Didn't *you* mention it?"

"No," Ruddabaugh said. "I figured it was none of my business. I've noticed curiosity don't pay big dividends in this neck of the woods. It's been my observation that if you want to get along with folks the best way of doing it—"

Durango snapped his cigarette into the fireplace with visible irritation. "Now look, Ruddabaugh! I don't want to call any man a liar, but there's a damn' sight more to this business than you're lettin' on. Forney comes to this place last night at ten o'clock. After a lot of loud talkin' in your bar, he notices the two Mex customers an' suggests adjourning to the back room. You two go back there, an' the barkeep sends the drinks. You talk in there till round eleven, yet all that talk—accordin' to you—was done by Forney about Karvel doing him out of his job an' about all he was fixing to do to even the score. Now," the marshal's sloe eyes glittered, "I'm not fool enough to swaller that. Either you're comin' clean or I'm puttin' a padlock on this place. Which is it goin' to be?"

The tavern boss met that hard regard unblinkingly. He even smiled a little, regretfully. "Sorry you're takin' it that way, Les. I've told you all I know about it." His hand shook a little bell he had lifted off the table. One of his house men came in, and he told the fellow to fix up a fire. "Legs are botherin' me again this morning," he said apologetically to Durango. "Every time the weather changes—"

"Ever contemplate how they'd feel in a prison?"

But Ruddabaugh only chuckled in his slow, good-natured way. "You're a rare one, Les—a rare one. Always lookin' on the sunny side of life. Just like an undertaker that I knew once over to Joplin; *he* was always a fella for making cheerful prophecies, too. I've often wondered . . . Why— aren't you feelin' well this morning, Les?"

The marshal *did* look a little queer. He seemed to pull himself together with an effort. "Never mind me," he muttered. "What were you talking about with that greaser you sent out for after Forney left last night?"

Ruddabaugh looked thoughtful. Then he chuckled. "Bandera? I had him over to ask about a couple of *santos* he was carving. He'd promised to have them ready by the last of the month and—"

Durango's curse stopped the flow of words. Durango's lips cut a half-circle gash across twisted, burnt-leather features. His voice loosed a passion-choked whisper, malignant, menacing.

"You're lyin', by God, an' I know it. When I can prove it I'm comin' back!" Without another word he stamped past Ruddabaugh. He went out the door and slammed it back of him.

Chapter 16

"STAND BACK!"

It was eleven-fifteen when Rush's borrowed bronc first brought him within sight of town. An impressive sight it was, too, with the green of scrub oak, spruce and hemlock, gaily interspersed with the pastel shades of adobe and stucco houses, with mine dumps showing in the distance like yellow and blue blotched ant runs against the looming hills, and down in the deepest hollow the warm, sympathetic orderliness of buff-tinted Spanish architecture where department stores, post office and depot set cheek by jowl with one another for all the world like a trio of judges caught napping in solemn conclave. Yonder, thrust in sweeping majesty against a turquoise sky, the sassafras yellow contour of a graceful arch rose in breath-taking lines just beyond a crowded intersection, giving regal entrance to Cement Canyon, along the sides of which more adobe and stucco houses perched like fat little toads in the sun.

Tyrone! Rush was glad enough to see it. Twice during the night he had been lost and ridden God knew how many miles out of his way. Several times he'd thought he caught the sound of some following horseman; but though he'd waited time and again, concealed in some dark thicket, no sign of pursuit had propelled itself across his vision.

His spirit still chafed at the thought of that final scene with Paw—at the way Paw'd shoved that rifle at him and told him to "git!" The daffy old coot! It made Rush burn to think of how Paw'd dropped that fellow—shot him off his horse without a chance. Trying to run off Clem like that, the fellow had sure got what he'd been asking for; but Rush would not have killed a *dog* so damned cold-bloodedly. What was the use in having law if a guy was going to do things that way? Showed the hair-trigger Paw was geared to; when he'd told Rush to "git!" Rush had sure known he meant business. At that he'd been prepared to argue the point—and would have except for that look he'd caught in Clementine's eyes. A gritty kid, by God! Might not be so bad having her round to fetch his slippers and cook his meals at that. He was no staunch advocate of double harness, but if he ever decided to change his mind and get hooked up to some skirt, Clem would be the kind he'd want to tie to.

Mostly, though, Rush's thoughts concerned themselves with Paw. Crotchety old devil. Like all the rest of the sun-addled, snake-bitten prospectors Rush had met. Crazy as a sway-backed bull—just as soon kill a man as look at him! No more regard for human life than a bullet.

Sure had a mine back there, though. Best damn ore Rush had ever clapped his eyes on. Looked as if Stevens hadn't been so batty after all—

But wait a minute. Stevens! Who the hell was Stevens?

He cudgeled his brains but could not figure out the man's identity. Stevens . . . Where had he heard that name? What had Stevens said? For a moment, it seemed as if he'd almost found a signpost on his backtrail.

But it was gone to blazes now all right. The name sure had sounded familiar on his tongue. Must be somebody he had known. Damn such a memory as would go back on a man the way his had. What the hell ailed him anyway? Could that gunshot wound Clementine had nursed him out of account for a thing like that?

He shook his head, muttering under his breath. It sure snarled a fellow's trail up plenty not to know who he was. He couldn't even remember if he'd been born round here or gravitated this way naturally. The country didn't seem in any way familiar. It was damn bad fix for a man to be in, though, no getting around that part. What if he'd made enemies round here? What if he had a feud on?

He stared about uneasily. He'd sure have to keep his peepers open; some gent might be layin' for him. Had—

Well, damnation! So that's who Stevens was! The desert rat he'd met that night in the Double Axe—the fellow who'd told him about that nonexistent gold rush! That was right. He recollected now coming out here with those burros; how he'd loaded them down with a lot of truck he'd thought birds with gold colic might have a use for. But where were they now— what had he done with them? Seemed as if he remembered them running away from him; but that might be false memory, something conjured from all the stories that he'd heard. Guys were always telling about some prospector's burro running off.

Another thing: what had he been doing before he'd met this Stevens? How had he been employed? Where? By whom? Had he quit, attracted by the lure of Stevens' yarn?

He'd met the desert rat in town; was he a town man? But no, that couldn't be. Yesterday he'd followed that kidnapper's tracks for miles. Town men couldn't read sign like that. Vaguely he had some notion he'd been working on a ranch. But what would he have been doing in town in such case? Had he been elected sheriff or something?

He shook his head again. As in the case of the origin of his gunshot wound, he didn't know about it. One thing emerged from the tangle, though; if he was new to this Burro country, he couldn't have made many enemies.

Somewhat easier in his mind, he relaxed a little in the saddle and looked around. This must be Tyrone, the town Clementine had mentioned. It looked as if he were coming in at the back door, sort of, cutting down this canyon. That looked like a road ahead—it was. Well traveled, too, by the sign.

He swung the borrowed horse into it and saw to the left in the yonder distance a solid row of connected adobe houses, one-story boxlike things, built for use and without adornment. A bunch of squalling kids were playing some kind of game that required a lot of noise just off to the side of them. Miners' kids, he guessed; the girl had said this was a mining town.

He wished to hell he had his burros and all that stuff packed on them. A fellow could peddle duffle like that without any trouble soon as news of Paw's discovery got round. Damned queer it hadn't got round already.

He grimaced, recalling Paw's handy talent with a rifle. Maybe that was how he'd come by that gunshot wound that had laid him up in the old rooster's packing-box cabin. He tried to think, to backtrack himself from effect to cause.

But he couldn't do it. At last, reluctantly, he turned his attention to the town, to the things around him.

Just ahead lay the plaza, a riot of color, looking more like a chunk of imported Spain than any

American mining camp. Gay serapes and straw sombreros agleam with glittering braid and silver; and some with tiny bells that jingled merry tunes. A laughing, gesticulating, jabbering throng, dark-hued of visage yet warm and vibrant, stimulating, with flashing teeth and the barbaric color schemes of clothing. Turquoise, topaz and fluorspar cast back the sun from ear lobes and chubby fingers; and lace mantillas vied in elegance with the bottle-glass gleam of men's boots.

Entering the square sprawled with Spanish somnolence about the park-enlivened plaza with its dusty trees and wire-railed aloofness, Rush saw to his right the rock-built front of the tan-stone Company building. A steady stream of dark-skinned men were passing in and out, and other streams were lined up, receiving slips of paper at a row of ground-floor windows on the right beneath the portico. Pay day at the mines, he thought, and tightened his belt reflectively. If he could get some kind of job . . . There ought to be room for a white man.

But first he'd hunt a saloon and wash some of this alkali out of his system. Ought to stop some place and take a look at his wound, too; it had been aching him considerably off and on these last few hours. This unaccustomed riding and yesterday's prowl across the hills might have opened it up or something.

He wanted to find a bed and sleep the clock around. But if this was pay day and he aimed to get a job, he ought to stop in at the Company office before the place closed up.

He'd get a drink and hurry back; the rest could wait till later. He'd sleep better, anyway, knowing he had a job.

He stopped a passing Mex and asked him where he could find a saloon. "Old Town, *señor.*" The man held up four fingers with a grin. "These many—can take your pick. *Seguro.*"

"An' where's Old Town?"

The man stretched out a swarthy arm, pointing down the road. "Go past the *juzgado.* Nex' road on the left."

Rush jogged on. He passed the butcher shop, Western Union, the Trading Company and bank. That was not their order; it was the way Rush's glance picked them out. The Bank of Tyrone was lined with tile—a temple built to Mammon.

He passed the hat-maker's shop, and the road made a quirk to the left, then angled right again. Straight west it led, and on the left Rush glimpsed the school, a three-storied affair of yellow brick looking big enough to hold all the kids in the state. It looked as if Burro Mountain Copper had built with an eye to the future. "Nothing tight about *their* style," he grunted.

On the right another canyon opened up. The houses there were spaced more comfortably, with grass and trees around them, and with a windmill showing above them farther up the canyon's slope.

A little further riding brought him to what he guessed must be the jail. "Justice Court," the name said: a squat, gray stucco building set well back from the road beyond a grove of ancient oak trees. There were three or four buggies hitched before it and cattle in a corral behind. A leather-faced man lounged to the left of the door with a wad of tobacco in his cheek and with his eyes fixed, brightly curious, upon Rush as he passed. Rush nodded and the fellow's head dipped briefly, but for a long way down the road Rush felt the fellow's keen regard burning hot against his back.

He came in time to the road off the left. A wide canyon, house-dotted, crossed with lanes and fences, cut a wide swath through pine-thatched hills. These were poorer houses, the homes of Mexicans and other foreign labor at the mines. Or so Rush judged by his glances at passing faces. Houses built like Paw's from crates and packing boxes, with roofs of ill-assorted bits of corrugated tin weighed down with stones and sod chunks. Here and there was a dwelling built from logs, and one place had a front yard of filled earth penned by a wall of cement and stone.

Rush stopped at the Broken Bucket, a rambling structure of yellow pine poles, and climbed stiffly from his horse. He dropped the reins across a rail and entered the cool, dim building.

There were half a dozen customers present, he saw when his eyes grew accustomed to the change of light. Mostly Mex, they bellied up to the bar in their white cotton clothes and tossed quips back at the barkeep. Rush found a corner table near the wall and gave his commands to a plump little morsel with raven hair, high cheek bones and a pair of scarlet lips, who smiled and rolled her eyes as she wheeled away for his tequila. But Rush was too worn to feel any interest in women.

He sprawled with his head on an arm thrown across his table, ignoring the things about him, conscious only of his overwhelming weariness and a tremendous desire for sleep. The girl had to shake him when she brought his drink. Rush gave her a silver dollar and said she could keep the change. She indicated a friendly willingness to sit with him, but he shook his head. He might feel frazzled as a three-day drunk, but he knew where to draw the line.

After she had gone, he swigged his cactus brew in a moody aloofness. The fiery tequila roused him somewhat from his lethargy, but even so he did not notice when it was that the white man with his two Mex friends came in; was not even aware of their presence till, abruptly warned by some sixth sense, he looked up and found them watching him from a table three feet away.

The Mexicans in their soiled white cotton clothing were no different in appearance from their countrymen at the bar. Yet their eyes had a glinting hardness, their long-fingered hands a leanness that were not in keeping with the look of the miners; and one fellow had a livid scar across a flat left cheek bone.

Their white companion was a rugged man whose stocky figure bulged the fabric of his dusty blue serge suit. He wore a flower-embroidered vest after the fashion of a gambler, with a massive gold-linked chain looped across its front. He was good-looking in a cold and arrogant way; his smooth-shaved cheeks were ruddy and his eyes showed a keen intelligence as they looked at Rush with a probing stare that was axe-like in its sharpness.

"Do I know you?" Rago asked.

The ruddy-faced man made no reply; nor did his regard swing off by a fraction. Rush said, more bluntly: "If I don't, would you mind lookin' some place else? I ain't partial to bein' stared at."

The stocky man's shoulders raised and dropped; and through the taproom's dim half-gloom Rush could see a queer expression of amusement that was more than half vindictive satisfaction change the set of the man's florid features. It struck Rush suddenly the man knew *him* and had sought this meeting deliberately.

His widened gaze took in again the man's two darker companions. Motionless, alert and fully awake upon the instant, Rago felt the swing of their tempers. Vaguely it was like some half-remembered scene from his past; he had that elusive impression. But it was the present he had to deal with. These men were here to get him; without knowing why, he was utterly convinced of this fact. The sultry warning was in that chilling atmosphere. A look of crystallizing purpose shone balefully from their eyes.

One by one he checked his chances, ruthlessly discarding them. The door giving onto the street was too far off. The way to the bar was blocked by the foot of one Mex thrown across the aisle. The nearest window was eight feet away; remote as Egypt if gun or knife came into play. But he had Paw's gun and he had this table, and if the break came he would use them.

The stocky man said: "My name is Haigler," and smiled very coolly, very thinly.

He looked as though that ought to mean something. And it did. Rush remembered with a start where he had heard that name before. The name last night had sealed a rider's fate; the girl had cried just before Paw had dropped the kidnapper: "He was takin' me to Haigler—!" Then Paw had fired.

Gently Rush pushed back his chair and came upright with a poised erectness, big hands empty at his sides. He hadn't expected to be able; when he was up he waited stiffly, his smoky eyes taking in the rebellious detail of Phil Haigler's darkened cheeks.

Haigler said: "Tom, get over by the bar. Pete—"

"You boys," Rush drawled, "will stay right where you are if you cotton to what is good for you."

Haigler's harsh words rode the quiet: "Get over by the bar. Goddam you—move!"

The left-hand Mex came out of his chair reluctantly. He eyed Rush with a straining care and began furtively to back up.

"Another step," snapped Rush, "an' you can have it."

The Mexican went stone-rigid. His pink tongue licked across dry lips.

"Damn you," Haigler lashed. "Get over there!"

But the man was done with moving. He seemed to know this. The gleaming of his ferret eyes betrayed it; a forecast of his breaking nerve was in that anxious brilliance, and when his hand stabbed suddenly beltward Rago let him have it. His gun was lifting in his hand when the life went out of him.

Even while that report was crashing thunder against the walls, Rush's left hand upended the table, jamming it into Haigler, spoiling the fellow's aim. Some place a woman screamed. Rush saw the second Mex, Pete, coming at him,

157

face hidden behind a blur of smoke, then out of it, nearer, clearer, like a doll's that had been left overnight in rain. It was a dying man Rush's lunge sprawled on the floor; a dead man that tripped him up, caroming him, off-balance, into Haigler, just as that cursing gentleman's gun rose clear of the table and exploded.

Powder-driven air beat hard against Rush's face, choking him, half blinding him, while waves of sound drummed fury from the walls and ricocheted like souls turned out of heaven. Rush slammed his pistol outward in a vicious downward arc that missed by inches. Haigler's weapon barked again. A jagged line of splinters churned up whitely on the bar as Haigler, snarling, dropped his gun and reached for Rago's throat.

Powder stench was like a smelter's breath and the whole room danced and shivered in a fog of curdled smoke. Rush drove Paw's pistol forward in another smashing arc; grinned maliciously at the sound and feel of meaty impact; cursed as the hard bright barrel sheared off Haigler's lifting shoulder. He had a fleeting impression of scuttling shapes plunging headlong through the building's shattered windows. Then the gun was wrenched from his hand and a man's snarled voice was shouting hoarsely in his ear: "You damn fool! Drop it, I say; *stand back*—stand back or I'll drill you!"

Chapter 17

"SOONER SEE MY DAUGHTER DEAD—"

Trudging through the moon-drenched night across the tumbled mountains, Paw said not a word. Nor did he discard his black, locked silence back at the cave-house. He sat there somberly nursing his rifle, hunched, a bitter, brooding shape, while Clementine, outwardly chastened but inwardly resentful, found occupation for her hands redding up the place and, that done, getting breakfast.

Paw gulped his food down without remark and tramped outside. In the entrance he crouched hunkered on his boot heels, staring out over the canyon like some angel of the "darker drink," obscure, unapproachable, with the Sharps cradled on his knees.

Clementine shuddered a little, seeing him crouched there that way. So he must have crouched last night when he dropped that fellow from his saddle. She guessed she'd remember *that* sight as long as ever she lived. Why did memory have to be so hateful?

She flashed a covert look through the open door to where the old man sat with his ready rifle, grim, unyielding, dour as his own gar soup.

She guessed Noah must have worn that kind of expression when he warned the ancients of the Great Deluge. But Noah had been different; he hadn't taken the law into his own hands when things hadn't gone the way he wanted them— *he'd* been satisfied to leave God's work to God. Paw was a sight too quick on the trigger. When Paw wanted something, you'd best to give it to him. Or else look out!

She wondered what he thought about, sitting there like a Holy Judgment. She wondered why he sat there with that rifle fixed so handy. Did he think Rush was coming back? Was he cached out there to get him—to drop him out of his saddle as he'd dropped that man he'd killed last night?

She felt suddenly inexplicably afraid.

They were at dinner when the sound of hoof-beats reached them. Paw stopped chewing on the instant, put down his knife and listened, bent forward, queerly tensed.

"Stay here," he ordered gruffly and, picking up the Sharps, slid sideways through the door. They were the first words he had spoken to her since that fellow had run off with her; and the way he said them showed he meant to be obeyed. She had a lifetime of his gruff ways behind her, eighteen years of loyalty; but she did not obey him now. Curiosity was a pushing force; and fear the rider might be Rush and that Paw'd gun him with the same cold fury he showed canyon rattlers turned her rebellious, defiant of his orders.

She tiptoed to the door. The hoof sound had grown much plainer. Paw squatted with the Sharps against a shoulder, peering downward, waiting, motionless as an Indian, his finger curled round the trigger.

The horse was coming more slowly, as though its rider were in no hurry or were not quite sure of the way. But Paw was patient. Like a god carved out of granite, he sat waiting with his rifle.

Clementine had a moment's wonder at herself. Was this she, peering over Paw's shoulder with such a crazy pounding heart? Why should she concern herself with this rider? Even if the man were Rush—what of it? What was there in that to make her feel so stealthy, anxious, jumpy? Was it really the possibility of the approaching horseman's being Rush that made her feel so queer?

She crept nearer, scarcely breathing, went perfectly still as Paw leaned lower, adjusted the focus of his rifle and waited with the stock against his cheek.

Her heart stopped in an agony of fear and indecision. The rider was just beyond the bend now. If it were Rush, she would jump Paw, startle him, spoil his aim. Not because it was Rush, she told herself, but because she didn't want Rush's death laid at her father's door.

A quick grunt came from Paw; the rifle wavered

in his hands. With a muttered imprecation he half rose to his feet, leaning farther forward, putting a hand to the cavern wall to steady himself as he peered . . .

Clementine, strangely agitated, stared across his shoulder. The horseman wasn't Rush—wasn't a man at all. It was a woman in man's store clothes with a hard round hat perched on her yellow curls!

Paw said: "That's far enough," and let her see his rifle.

Clementine could see her staring up at him, her frown giving way to a cajoling smile. "Can you tell me where the Lubbocks live?"

"I'm Lubbock—"

"Are you really?" She seemed to be studying him, or maybe making up her mind to something. She said abruptly: "May I come up? I've—"

"Stay right where you are," Paw warned, "or I'll spoil that complexion for you. Who are you? What're you doin' up here?"

The girl in the hard hat hesitated. "I'm Estrella Proctor—"

"Proctor! One of that Y Bench crowd?"

"My father owns the Y Bench—yes. But—"

"You turn that nag around an' git the hell out of there before I do you a hurt!" Paw roared. "No goddam Y Bench—"

Clementine saw the girl put her hands to her ears till Paw's private cusswords were exhausted.

162

But she had the grit to stay where she was, and Clementine, pushing forward, from beside Paw called: "Did you come over yere to hold palaver with me?"

Proctor's daughter drew a breath of relief. "As a matter of fact, I did. If you'll come down, we can talk more—"

"She'll stay right where she is," Paw growled, "an' you turn that bronc around an' git before I do you a mischief. Since when has the Y Bench taken to callin' at Maverick Canyon? You tell that horse-thievin' father of yours he can't pull no wool over *my* eyes. Go on—git home an' tell him that! You tell him the next Y Bencher I catch round here will sure git planted where I find him."

"Please! Your feud with father doesn't interest me. I've come over here to do you a favor and—"

"Favor!" Paw snorted. "I guess so! Like that favor your ol' man did me yesterday, I reckon! You git out of here now before I come down an' pack you out personal."

He advanced threateningly toward the trail, but Proctor's daughter stood her ground. "These heroics simply don't impress me," she said scornfully. "You may scare the likes of Bronc Forney, but I've got sense enough to know it's a lot of bluster. This country's civilized; people don't go around shooting one another any more—it's out of date. Grudges are settled in the courts—"

"Mebbe that's where your ol' man settles *his* grudges," Paw growled darkly.

She flushed angrily. "I've come over here at a considerable effort to try and do you a favor. If you don't care to hear what I've got to say, it's entirely on your own head." Clementine could see the contempt of her curling lips and felt ashamed for Paw that he could treat a lady so. She was tempted to put in her oar again, but just as she would have spoken the girl said: "It doesn't matter two pins to me one way or the other; but my father wants the water rights of this canyon and he's prepared to stoop to a pretty low trick to get them. I don't want to see him victimize—"

"He'll have to get up pretty damn early to pull any victim stunts on me," Paw scoffed. "An' you can tell him that I said so."

"Are you going to listen to me or aren't you?" Proctor's daughter said haughtily.

"Go ahead if you got to—swing your jaw an' get it over."

For a moment Clementine thought the girl would leave. She half turned her horse, exasperated; then some thought appeared to override the impulse. She turned in her saddle to look up at Lubbock with resentment written plain across her features. "I ought—as Dad would say—to let you stew in your own juice," she told him. "Anyone who's so bull-headed—"

"Never mind all that. Just spill your guts and be

on your way. The quicker you get out of here the better I'll be likin' it."

"There's a man named Karvel working for the Y Bench," she said with a quickness showing her repugnance for what she was about to do, yet with a vehemence that told she meant to accomplish whatever mission had brought her so far off her father's range. "Knowing how badly Dad wants these canyon water rights, he made a proposition. For a consideration he proposes to marry your girl and then, in the event you should happen to meet with an accident—"

Paw's snort was a measure of his contempt. "My 'girl,' as you call her," he said sardonically, "is pretty damn choosy what kind of pelican she takes up with. Takes after me that way—we don't truck around with riffraff. As fer me meetin' with any 'accident,' your man Karvel ain't up to pullin' no such miracle."

The false expression of amusement left Paw's face; left it bleakly, uncompromisingly hostile. "You tell this Karvel if he wants to go on livin' he better steer plum clear of this canyon—an' that goes for the rest of your crowd. Now you clear out of here. Pull your freight."

Proctor's daughter looked as if she wanted to chew him. If looks could have killed, Paw would have withered on the spot. "After going so far out of my way as to come over here and warn you—"

"Don't bother paradin' that fancy for my

benefit," Paw growled. "I know what brought you over here. I been weaned a week or two. You can set your mind at rest; your friend ain't hookin' up with nobody from this section. I'd sooner see my daughter dead than married to a goddam Y Bencher!"

Chapter 18

DURANGO MAKES A PROPHECY

Rush stood perfectly still.

For the space of a dozen heartbeats those snarled words roweled through his mind; it took him that long to calm down and lose his hot emotion. Then he saw Phil Haigler going back three jerky steps, standing with his eyes fixed on the speaker, with his big fists hanging like mallets at his sides and with his dropped gun lying on the floor between his feet. Half wheeled that way, he made a wide and bulky shadow against the bar.

"What was this bird tryin' to pull here, anyway?"

Rush thought he caught a smile of slyness faintly curling the corners of Haigler's mouth. "Have you looked around?" Haigler said, and swung a bitter glance upon the sprawled, unmoving shapes of his late companions. "Looks like the evidence ought to speak pretty plain for itself. When this damn fool yanked his smokepole I was talking to the waitress, not paying him any mind. These two boys, I guess, must have seen the play from scratch. They pitched in to help me; tried to grab him . . ." Haigler shrugged.

"Killing folks seems to come natural to him. Maybe he figures Mexicans don't count."

When he was sure that Haigler had finished, Rush shot a quick look at the speaker. He was an ugly, pockmarked man of a saddle-whipped leanness and with a skin like parboiled leather. There was a badge pinned on his vest and a look of authority in his stare. There was something else in that reticent stare, too, but Rush couldn't make it out.

"Know him?" the star-packer asked, and when Haigler shook his head, brought his glance back to Rago sharply. "Got anything to say?"

"About what?"

"You might talk about these killin's for a start."

"Justifiable homicides," Rush said coolly. "A man's got a right to defend himself—"

"You got a queer idea of defense—"

"You ain't heard my side of this business yet."

The star-packer eyed him coldly. "What *is* your side of it?"

"You figurin' to arrest me?"

"I reckon I am."

"I'll save my story for the trial then."

"Tough monkey, ain't you?" The tinbadge sneered. "What handle are you packin' these days?"

"I haven't had any occasion to change the one I got born with. My name's—"

Into the awkward pause the man with the star

168

said knowingly: "Pick a good one while you're at it."

Rush scowled. He said, "My name's Ed Cotton."

"Cotton, eh?"

And Haigler said: "I think he's lyin', Marshal."

There was plain agreement in the marshal's sloe-eyed stare. "Cowhand, ain't you? What out-fit are you punchin' for?"

"Not with any at the moment. I been ridin' round, sort of lookin' things over—"

"Yeah. I've met your kind before—grub-line riders; drifters. You've drifted into the wrong place this time, Cotton. Just hand me that gun—butt forward."

Rush's glance raked the room. No chance. He blew a sigh through his teeth and gave the marshal his weapon. There was nothing else he *could* do. The marshal's gun had been taking his picture for the last three minutes.

"I'd like to talk to a lawyer . . ." He stopped, seeing Haigler's grin.

The lawman said: "I'll see you get one—in time for the trial. No sense in runnin' up the town's expenses beforehand. Be several weeks before your case comes up. How long you known Bronc Forney?"

"Never heard of him—"

"I'll take you round to see him after a while. Maybe the look'll refresh your memory. Any fella—"

"Say, look here, Durango," muttered Haigler suddenly. "I believe I know who this hombre is. There's a fella been prowlin' the hills around here lately. Fiori was sayin' something the other night about meeting him. Told Fiori his name was Rush Rago, but the description sure fits this fella like a glove."

Rush saw them exchange significant glances. "What the hell is this—a frame up?"

The star-packer wheeled with a scowl. "Don't use that word in connection with the law in this town, hombre. Les Durango don't frame nobody. I give a man a square break always, an' if he's innocent he's got nothing to worry about; not a damn thing—see?"

He looked at Haigler. "If you know where Fiori is, go fetch him. Maybe he can identify this—"

The shake of Haigler's head was slow; was regretful. "I ain't seen Buck for quite a spell—since I was talkin' to him in the Wheel House Bar the other night when he was tellin' me about this fellow."

"He ought to be round here some place. His bronc's outside."

Durango's glance came up with a sudden narrowness as the Broken Bucket's proprietor came hurrying in. Durango said: "Know this fella?" and jerked a hand at Rush. With a puzzled look the newcomer shook his head. "No sabe."

"Ever see him before?"

Another shake of the head.

"Well, get these stiffs moved out of here," the marshal muttered with a hard look at the two dead Mexicans. "Have somebody pack 'em over to the undertakin' parlors; there's got to be a inquest." He brought his glance to Haigler. "I expect you'll be preferrin' charges . . ."

"No," murmured Haigler unexpectedly. "I guess not. You won't be needin' me in this, anyway; you got an open-an'-shut case. Without justification or warning, this bird yanks his gun an'—"

"According to *your* version," Rush put in. "Mine's goin' to sound considerably different."

Haigler flung him a caustic look and returned his regard to the lawman. "As I was saying, you won't have any trouble getting a case against this drifter. There was half a dozen fellows in here when—"

The marshal's eyes were raking the emptied room with a pointedness not even Haigler could ignore. Haigler said: "Never mind. You stick him in the cooler anyway. If nobody comes forward to testify, I'll get into it for you."

Slyness edged the marshal's regard. "You won't be gettin' into it for me," he said. "You're in it now."

Haigler wheeled, the expression of his roan cheeks hot, belligerent. There was a nervous

171

movement in his chest as if he bottled an emotion that was threatening to explode within him. His burly shoulders hunched.

But Durango grinned at him coldly. "I guess you know where I stand."

There was some hidden significance in the words, for Rush saw the way Haigler's eyes flashed. But he got no time to think about it, for Durango told him curtly: "Outside, Cotton. An' don't try any tricks."

Haigler, with a protest on his lips, half wheeled round to follow them; but something stayed the impulse and they left the place without him. "Get on your horse," the marshal said, and pulled his own bronc's reins from the rack.

A keen, hard brightness showed in his eyes as Rush swung into the saddle. But he said no word till they reached the jail and swung down, with the feel of the big leather-faced tobacco-chewer's glance upon them. It was the man who had waved to Rush when he went past—the man who had watched him out of sight.

This man and the marshal now looked at each other knowingly. "Same fella?" Durango drawled, and the tobacco-chewer nodded.

"Same guy."

Durango said: "What you doin' with Fiori's horse, Cotton?"

Rush started. He'd forgotten he rode a horse he had no claim on. If this horse belonged to Fiori, that meant Fiori was dead—was the hombre Paw had shot.

He felt an impulse to whirl the bronc and make a run for it, but a quick look into the marshal's watching eyes dropped the notion stillborn. He racked his brains for some reasonable explanation—vainly.

Durango said: "I guess that's one of them things you're savin' to spring at the trial," and laughed unpleasantly. "D'you know what I think? I think you killed Fiori jest like you killed Forney an' them two oilers."

Rush could not meet that baleful, challenging stare. Events had trapped him nicely. There was no out that he could see. He couldn't tell this star-packer Fiori *was* dead; that Paw had dropped him without a chance. Such a statement would be a poor return for the way Paw's girl had nursed him when he'd been down with that gunshot wound.

The marshal said: "Guess you better start buildin' a gallows, Bransen. This bird's got all the earmarks."

Bransen's laugh held anticipation. Rush could not repress a shiver. But he said evenly enough: "I wouldn't go countin' my chickens till they hatched if I was you."

Durango looked at him curiously. "They'll hatch, like enough," he said.

Chapter 19

A PRETTY KETTLE OF FISH

The night following the afternoon of Rush's arrest was moonless. The myriad stars peering down from the sky's black vault did little to illuminate mountain trails, yet a rider on a walking horse bore ever deeper into the Burros, picking his way after the manner of one familiar with the country; a solitary horseman clad in black and with his face obscured behind the folds of a black bandana.

He showed no hurry, no hesitation; shot no questing glances right or left. It was not a stealthy progress; save for the kerchief-muffled features, the man might have been a cowman returning home after a night in town. He came to Iron Creek, followed it north to its junction with Maverick Canyon and, still at the leisurely pace, swung into the canyon.

He might have been riding to some fixed rendezvous with Paw for all the anxiety one could have detected. There was no sign of worry about him; he rode with the quiet sureness, the efficiency and casualness of a man to whom all things are possible, as aloof from care and the dangers of his undertaking as though he sat home reading with his feet propped on a hassock.

Yet there *was* danger in his mission—plenty; and not the least of it was the danger of being kept out after daylight. And there was danger from the trail leading up to that cave-house; he understood its vicissitudes from careful, glass-aided observation. He'd thought for a spell that the business which had taken him out tonight could be concluded in town . . . perhaps in the place of his own choosing. But the old man, patient watchfulness had discovered, never came to town; few Tyrone men had ever heard of him. This present trip was the fortuitous result of circumstance; a trek to Maverick Canyon that, until last night, he had not seen in the cards. It was indicated now, though—definitely. This meeting had to take place; and quickly, before someone of those gold-hunting nitwits rubbed Gable out for his mine. Before, he thought with a grimace, that fathead Durango got some lucky hunch and stumbled on a clue to Forney's killer.

He shifted, trying to ease his aching joints of saddle cramp; kneed Fiori's horse to a faster pace. Dawn must not catch him out and he must get this bumble-gaited nag reimpounded before the livery-keeper missed him.

Not many men having a working knowledge of Lubbock's character would have cared to risk bearding him in his own bailiwick; this rider was looking forward to it. The possibility of Paw sitting up with a rifle rather tickled his sardonic sense of humor. If Paw were catching forty winks he'd have to be got up, for the man on Fiori's commandeered horse had no intention of Paw's not knowing with whom he was dealing. This bandana was to keep other people from knowing.

From time to time the solitary horseman lifted increasingly more deeply scowling glances to the star-shot sky. It looked as if a moon were rising. He hadn't thought to check an almanac. Something, seemed like, was always bound to be left out of even the best laid plans.

He stopped Fiori's horse just south of the canyon's bend. He had wanted Lubbock to see that horse; but reflection had assured him it would be sheer folly to tackle Paw's cliff-trail a-horseback. That being the case, there was no point in heralding himself with hoof sound.

He left the bronc on trailing reins, pushing swiftly, quietly forward, pausing briefly to take stock of things when he came to the foot of the trail. There was a scud of cloud up there, and the bright shine on its fluffy edges hinted that he could count on the moon's appearance very shortly. Perhaps, after all, it would be smarter to wait till the moon came out before trying his luck on this climb. It would be unfortunate if he tried it in the dark this way and some unpredictable sound should warn Paw of an alien's presence and Paw should squirt the trail with lead. Let

Paw once see who was coming and there'd be no bark from the rifle.

The man grinned mirthlessly. No, Paw'd not shoot if he saw him.

It would be a sight less risky, though, if he could somehow lure Lubbock into coming down . . .

He shook his head regretfully. No chance of that. The recent peregrinations of the would-be claim-jumpers must have sharpened the old man's wits to too keen an edge for him to fall for any ordinary ruse. Any complex plan would use too much time. He *must* be back in town ere dawn. To be seen—

He cut loose of his thoughts abruptly, his body stiffening, his head canted in an attitude of listening. There was somebody on that trail. He knew the sound of a boot-kicked stone when he heard it; there was somebody up there ahead of him!

He was easing his gun free of leather when the moon broke away from its cloud.

Joe Karvel was nobody's fool. He was a far-seeing man, a thinking man, and master of himself upon all occasions. No bear's-tail swing had propelled him into this predicament; when he decided to cross up his partners in the Lubbock claim-jumping program, he did it knowing full well how hell-bent they'd be to plant him. That sort of danger did not weigh too heavy on his spirit; he had proved in past experiences his ability to take care of himself. Having no fear of either of them singly, he had taken steps to see they didn't gang up on him. A little vacation from home pastures was in order; he told Cowles Proctor the morning Proctor fired Bronc Forney that he was getting to work on that water deal, saddled up his private horse and set off with three days' rations.

He camped the first night near the head of Maverick Canyon and spent a deal of time studying Lubbock's layout through a pair of Y Bench glasses. Next evening, knowing that the moon would be late in rising, he deemed the time was ripe to put his plan to the test. The plan was simple. He would, under cover of the night's thick gloom, work down the canyon to a handy distance from the cliff-trail's start. There he would wait around till it seemed reasonable to suppose the old man would have gone to bed. Then he would climb the trail, as softly as it could be managed, and, arrived at where Lubbock's rifle would prove no asset to its wielder, he would play the part of a lost prospector and knock upon the old man's door. What happened after that would depend, of course, on circumstance.

He lounged a long while in darkness at the foot of the cave-house trail. To most men it would have been a lonesome vigil, a time keen-

fraught with danger—with jumpy agitations; a time wound up almost certainly with a too early tackling of the trail.

But not for Karvel. Being of a thoughtful turn of mind, and of a reflective, philosophical nature, he occupied the wait with rumination, pondering what he knew of the girl who was to play such an important role in his winning of that hundred thousand dollars.

She sure was a damned good looker, he thought dispassionately. He'd seen her that afternoon through the glasses. She'd been sitting at the cavern entrance with the old man's .30-.30. It shouldn't be *too* much of a chore making love to a dame like that. Of course she was just a kid, but . . . Lots of Mex kids married early; he guessed the legal aspect of the business could be made to stand up solidly enough. Had anyone told him Clementine was going on nineteen he'd have called him a liar; she certainly didn't look it.

He wondered where the hell she had gone to. It kind of slowed up his plans a little, her going off like that. It certainly had surprised him, her coming abruptly down the trail that way. He'd seen her pretty plainly through the glasses; "stealthy" was the way he'd have described her expression, and she'd kept looking back up the trail as if she were nervous. He'd thought maybe the old coot had read her a riot act about something and she was going off some place to have a good cry.

But that had been a bum guess—the crying part, anyway. He'd seen her some ten minutes later—about two-thirty that would have been—coming out of a little side canyon on a burro and leading another. The second had a pack on. The old man was sending her off some place with ore.

That guess, too, had been disproved when, around five o'clock, the old man had come out of the cave-house, scowling. He'd stood in the entrance bellowing and, when that hadn't brought her running, had gone storming down the trail in search of her. A vain search, too, by the look of him; Karvel had watched him climb back up the trail looking as mean as a digger Injun.

Maybe, Karvel thought, she had run off.

He couldn't see why she would, though. She might have gone to visit someone, some neighbor girl off in the hills somewhere—maybe Nettie Klepshoe over on Willow Creek. But why the extra burro? That, considering its pack, tended to confirm the notion she was pulling her freight.

He certainly hoped such was not the case. Her going off that way might throw a wrench in the works. She *would* have to pull a fit of temperament right now! Of course, in a way, he was just as well satisfied to have her away for a spell—just so she came along back when he was ready for her.

But first things first. Right now his business was with Lubbock.

Karvel glanced at the sky. About time he was getting up the trail if he aimed to get there in darkness. The damn moon would be coming up . . . It would be shining now if it weren't for that edge of cloud.

He set off up the trail.

Despite his reluctance to be caught in moon-glare, he took it easy. He had this need for caution. He must not rouse the old man prematurely. To advertise his presence before he reached that door might tend to be embarrassing—might even get his light blown out. He entertained a lively regard for the old man's shooting talent. He knew nothing of Haigler's recent antics nor of Fiori's sudden end, but, while scouting the place one day with Forney, he had seen old Lubbock drop a ground squirrel at three hundred paces by splashing lead off a rock.

He'd no inclination to have Lubbock trying any of that with him.

Halfway up, a loose pebble turned beneath his boot and went clattering into the canyon. It didn't make much noise, but in that vast New Mexican silence it seemed to Karvel as loud as the report of a gun. With a smothered oath he stood still, listening. The stillness was even greater than before—almost absolute; "breathless" was the word that came to Karvel's mind. It *did* have that hushed, kind of expectant air about it. A definite feel of watching eyes swung Karvel's torso half around; his glance was knife-sharp as it stabbed the crouching shadows of the trail.

The moon took that moment to break from its bed of cloud; the change in visibility was like the throwing of a light switch. A whisper of sucked-in breath marked Karvel's reaction. With narrowed stare intent, fixed on the trail below, he eased his body downward and sank like a bit of magic into the shadow of a spruce.

A man was on the trail down there—one might have said an apparition; but Karvel didn't believe in ghosts. A man snatched bodily from the pages of the past. That was how his mind translated what he saw. A man in a black Prince Albert with a tall black beaver on his head and a mask across his face. Had this been twenty years ago, and along the run of the Overland Stage, Karvel would have taken no second thought on the matter; he'd have gone about his business.

But it was not twenty years ago. The stage-robbing era was past. This was Maverick Canyon, an empty, rock-ribbed place where no man lived but Lubbock; and if yonder figure were Lubbock's, Karvel would undertake to eat him, Prince Albert, beaver hat and all.

He saw the man's hand reach inside the coat and caught the gleam of metal. Quietly he got his own gun out, then with a grunt reholstered it. This was no time for gunplay. One shot and Lubbock—

Karvel's lips streaked in a sudden grin.

Jove! that fellow couldn't have come in handier for his need. Here was a chance dropped in his lap that beat his own indifferent scheme four ways from the joker. Yon buck in the flapping Prince Albert could prove a godsend if he worked him right.

The thing now was to get posthaste to Lubbock. Get Lubbock out of bed and . . .

Swiftly, but with an admirable caution, Karvel resumed his interrupted climb. No stone must turn beneath his boot again; nothing must give that man below him further warning. He must reach and rouse Lubbock without delay, and meantime, if the gods were good, that fellow down yonder would do considerable thinking before he started up the trail.

About one thing Karvel had to be careful; he must not let the masked man see him. *That* hombre might not be so particular about a little noise.

Fast as he moved, it was tedious work. There were places where he had to get down on his belly and crawl. Other places, where the trail was bad, he needed every ounce of courage his heart could get a pump on. If it hadn't been for the constant danger of the man below catching sight of him, the trip would have been a cinch. But as things were he had need of all his patience, all his resource.

But he made it; he reached the cave-house door without an outcry. Flat on his belly, he reached out a hand and softly tapped at its bottom.

Night's silence took a keener edge—even the insects seemed to have stopped short their crazy chorus. There was not a sound in all the world . . .

"Who's there?" a voice queried guardedly. "That you, Clem?"

Karvel said, with his mouth pressed against the door: "I'm a stranger, mister. Keep your voice down—there's a guy with a gun on the trail."

The moments crept by.

When Karvel could contain himself no longer, he said desperately: "For God's sake open up! I come up here to warn you, but I didn't bargain to get shot. That bird's comin' up here!"

"That's tough."

"Mean to say you're goin' to leave me out here—me, without no gun? Gawdlemighty, fella! What am I goin' to do?"

"That's your problem," came Lubbock's soft chuckle. "Might try sproutin' wings."

The pad of bare feet announced the old fool's withdrawal.

Chapter 20

SURPRISE

Karvel, in his diagnosis of Clementine's odd flight, was partly right. He was right in assuming the likelihood of a lecture by the old man having driven her from the shack. Paw had jumped from his silence with a vengeance. With a bleak glance and the voice of Gabriel he had told her what she was—"runnin' off with a sneakin' brush-popper!" Rush Rago'd known the moment he'd read the sign that she'd been carried off against her will; had taken the trouble to make the fact plain to Paw. But Paw had seen the circumstances more clearly; Paw's knowledge of mankind's ways had given him an insight not vouchsafed to others. With quivering cheek, with twisted mouth and bitter eye, he'd spoken of "brands for the burning." With the look of Smith, the Prophet, he'd declared damningly: "The Scriptures put a name to the likes of you! Where's your pride, girl? Gawdlemighty! that Proctor wench knew you better'n I'd have guessed!"

He'd said much more and, finally, slamming the door behind him, he'd gone tramping out to his mine. Clementine sat where he'd left her for a long time, cowering there, white-cheeked, miserable, rebellious. It was rebellion finally won. Stormy-eyed, hurt, resentful of all the unjust accusations he had flung at her, she'd got to her feet with her mind made up. She'd not stay there any longer. If that was what he thought of her, he could have the place to himself and cook his own damn grub!

Leaving the old Sharps in the cave, she hurried down the cliff-trail. She would go to Tyrone. She knew where two of Rago's burros were, for she'd caught them and penned them up. She would take them to him; one still had its pack and perhaps he'd be glad to get it. She would go to him anyway. Maybe she could cook his meals— could keep his house swept out. Leastaways, he could tell her what to do; he knew the world— he'd traveled.

She thought of that time he'd grabbed her, snatched a kiss; and the sun suddenly seemed mighty hot.

But her intention did not falter. Rush might kiss her some, she guessed, but he'd not call her what she'd just been called and be forever ranting of *brands for the burning, abandoned baggages* and those other awful things that had come off Paw's tongue. And if Rush's advances got a little rough, she expected she could stand it. Anyway, she could always pull her freight; she wasn't obliged to stay with him. She allowed a good, strong, healthy girl could manage some way.

It was a little after six when she got to town, and supper fires were pouring smoke from its chimneys. It was the first time she'd ever been there, and she looked about with interest.

It sure was a pretty place, but awful crowded. Looked as if the whole world must have moved to Tyrone; she had never seen so many people in her life. "What's goin' on yere?" she called to a red-shirted fellow just ahead of her.

He looked round and pulled off his hat. His glance went to her burros and then came back in frank admiration to her face. "Durango's done caught the town a murderer," he said, and grinned up at her as if that were something pretty funny.

"Who's Durango?"

"Gosh sakes, don't you know *Durango?* He's the marshal. He's grabbed Bronc Forney's killer—caught him tryin' to carve up Haigler at the Broken Bucket this noon. Goin' to be some fun round here tonight."

Haigler's name took some of the healthy color from her cheeks. But it caught at her attention. "Phil Haigler?" And when he nodded she asked: "What are they fixin' to do to him?"

"Who—Haigler? Nothin'. This—"

"I mean the other man—the one the marshal caught."

"Oh. Him? Reckon some of the boys are goin' to have a necktie party," he said lightly, his eyes going over her with a deepened interest. "You must be new round here. Where you stayin'? Got anything on for tonight?"

She didn't catch the drift of the fellow's questions; hardly heard them. She said: "What was the murderer tryin' to carve Phil Haigler up for?"

"Search me. Some kinda grudge, I guess. Shot up two of Phil's Mex friends an' was gettin' set to bash Phil's light when Durango grabbed him."

"Humph," she commented. "Too bad he didn't wait a spell," and frowningly kicked the burros into motion.

An odd light marked the fellow's eyes as he stared after her. With a thoughtful look he put his hat on, then called impulsively: "You forgot to mention where-at you was stayin'. Good picture at the show tonight—Lillian Gish. How 'bout you an' me goin'?"

"No, thanks," she frowned across her shoulder. "I got one guy sparkin' me now, an' one's a-plenty."

Clementine and her burros made a quaint trio as they wandered round taking in the sights. All this was new to the girl, and she stared fascinated at the gay-colored buildings, the jostling throngs, the shop windows with their garish display of merchandise. Blue eyes bright and wide, she reveled in the freedom that permitted her to rove at will, giving her at last the longed-for chance to rub shoulders with these things that all her life she'd dreamed of. The world might be a wicked place as Paw had often told her, but it sure was mighty fetching. The immensity of the place, its smells and noise and hustle, all were food to her starved senses. She poked round most an hour before her stomach, rousing her to the need of more substantial grub, set her hunting for an eating place. She finally found one down in Old Town next door to the Wheel House Bar.

She hitched her burros to the snorting post and pushed her way inside. Golly Moses! but the place was packed. She did eventually find a seat at a table with three miners. They smelled of sweat and dirt and, with their grime-stained, beard-stubbled faces, were hardly the sort of supper company most girls would care to eat with; but Clementine was used to sweat and there'd been plenty of dirt on Paw nights when he'd come dragging to the table. She told the waitress what she wanted and asked how much they were going to charge her and scowled at the girl's smiling answer. "That's a powerful lot of money," she said, grimly counting it from the horde Paw'd stored in the coffee can. "You must be awful rich."

The miners grinned, and the girl said she only worked there and that nobody'd know it from what they paid their help. This was Greek to

Clementine, but the food was good and when it came she tackled it with relish.

She was halfway through her meal and the miners all were smoking when a chance remark of one of them jounced through the girl's preoccupation. "That saddle tramp's sure goin' to take the jump," he said; and one of his companions remarked that the fellow "didn't look like no murderer" to him. The third man said he'd like to know what the bird had had on Haigler. "Like to see someone give that cocky pussyfoot a trimmin'—he's too blinkin' smart by far."

"Funny thing," the first man said, "about Durango gettin' there so prompt-like. Fellow'd almost think he'd timed it. He's a slick one, right enough. Ever hear about that rancher he dropped over at El Paso ten-twelve years ago? 'F there hadn't been some string-pullin'—"

"There'll be string-pullin' tonight, all right. They'll swing that Rago higher'n a kite!"

"You reckon Durango'll try an' stop it?"

"Not him. He knows which side of his bread—"

"Hell! That jail wouldn't hold a ground-squirrel!"

"Held Rago pretty well this afternoon—"

"Ain't nobody tried to bust him out. You'll see. Wait'll some of that crowd from the Y Bench gets to town. Forney may not've been too popular with his hands, but—"

"Y Bench won't get a look-in. Haigler's been throwin' his jaw all over town; got a bunch of damfools all in a lather over these killin's. Claims this Rago pelican killed Forney and Fiori as well as the two greasers."

"Well, if you was to ask me," one of the others said, "I'd say I wouldn't put it past this Haigler to have killed Forney and Fiori himself. They been mixed up in somethin' together lately. I was talkin' to Ed Grimes what runs the livery. He says Haigler's had Fiori out in the hills . . ."

Clementine was in no way interested in where Phil Haigler had had Fiori. All her thoughts, all the rush of her young emotions were concentrated definitely on the one main fact of these men's conversation. Rush Rago was in jail, charged with having killed at least one man that she knew very well he hadn't killed—Fiori. Nor did she believe for an instant he had killed the Y Bench super. She said, without pausing to think how her interest might be construed by these rough men: "What makes them think this stranger killed Fiori?"

The men regarded her curiously, and for a moment no one said anything. Then the tall fellow offered: "I reckon it's because this stranger come in on Fiori's horse an' nobody's seen Fiori since a couple nights back. May not mean—"

"Why, that marshal fellow's a fool!" she exclaimed indignantly. "Rush never killed that consarned Fiori. My Paw done that, an' I seen him. An' far as that goes it served him right!"

She met their interested regard with flushed cheeks, her eyes defiant, her full breasts heaving with the excitement roused in her by the thought of Rush under padlock. "Where-at is this marshal, anyhow? I allow I got to auger with him pronto."

The tall man looked at his companions oddly. "An' who might you be, Miss?" he asked.

"Clementine—if it's ary of your business." She was shoving back her chair, in a lather to get out of the place, when the tall man laid a hand upon her arm.

"Clementine what?"

"Ain't it, though?" she said, and before he could puzzle out that one she was on her feet, her arm jerked free, and heading for the door.

There weren't so many people on the street now. "Prob'ly eatin'," Clementine guessed. But while she was unknotting Rush's two burros from the tie-rack, a Mexican woman waddled past, staring curiously over her shoulder. "Hey!" said Clementine. "Where-at kin I find the marshal?"

She was used to being stared at now; nearly all the women eyed her, no doubt taken with the man's patched clothing she had on.

The Mexican woman shrugged. Her smile revealed a flash of teeth. "No sabe," she said, and made her earrings dance, so emphatic was her head-shake.

Clementine stopped the first white man she saw and asked again.

"Durango?" The fellow scratched his head. "Most usually about this time, ma'am, you'll find him puttin' on the nose-bag. Right next door— the Wheel House Bar."

"Hold these confounded canaries fer me, will you?" She thrust the ropes upon him and hurried into the building he had pointed to.

It was pretty well patronized, and a kind of startled hush came over the place when it was discovered this was a girl togged out in ragged Levi's and cotton shirt. "You lookin' fer someone, Miss?" the barman nearest her asked.

"I'm huntin' Durango, the marshal. He round yere any place?"

A dark spare man with a face like parboiled leather appeared from a group at the bar's far end. He came toward her with a rider's lean hipped grace, unhurried, sloe eyes friendly but inscrutable.

"I'm Durango."

"Oh! You were out to our place once—"

"Was I?" His regard went blank, skeptical. "Sure you ain't mixin' me with—"

"Don't you remember me? I'm Lubbock's girl—Clementine."

"Don't know any Lubbock. You're off on the wrong foot, Miss," he said, with a rolling glance taking in the bystanders' interest. "If there's anything I can do for you, though . . . Here—I'll walk down to my office with you. This ain't no place fer a woman."

He piloted her from the bar and onto the street, his hold upon her arm discouraging protest. But once outside, Clementine said: "See here. You got a fella in your jail that hadn't ort to be there. Rush Rago is his name. I hear you got him jugged fer a killin'. I want to tell you he never killed Fiori—my Paw done that. Fiori tried to run off with me, but Paw catched up with him."

She paused to eye him anxiously. "That's the truth—it's true as Gospel. You believe me, don't you?"

"Hold on a minute now," Durango said. "Let me get this straight. You claim your Paw shot Buck Fiori? Where'd this happen? When?"

"Night before last in Lost Valley up in the Burros. Fiori catched me in the canyon an' made me go with him. Paw catched up, so mad he couldn't see straight, an' shot Fiori off his horse." She took a big breath. "You better let Rush Rago go. He didn't hev no part in it."

"An' your father's name is Lubbock, is it?"

"You know damn well it is! You was up to Maverick Canyon visitin' him not two months back. I seen him give you some of his ore. Are you goin' to turn Rago loose or ain't you?"

The marshal thought about it. "Where'd he

hang an' rattle night 'fore last when Bronc Forney was gettin' his light snuffed?"

"He was up in Lost Valley with Paw—"

"All night?"

"Not *all* night—no. But he wouldn't have had no time . . . Say, look here; this fella's been fortin' up with us an' he's all right. Only thing, Paw's got it in his head Rush is after his dang mine. But Rush don't know ary thing about minin'—helps his burros carry their packs," she added, as if that explained everything.

"I see," Durango murmured. "How come—" he shot a quick look at her from under frowning brows—"how come you to be so all-fired sure this bird I got in the can is Rago?"

"Why, the whole town's buzzin' with it! They're figgerin' to string him up tonight, the crazy lunkhaids. They're sayin' you won't turn a hand to stop 'em—"

"Mebbe," the marshal said with a sudden tightening of the lips, "you better come down an' look this hombre over. Name he give me was Cotton—Ed Cotton."

She said impatiently: "You don't want to pay no mind to what he says. *He's* apt t' tell you anything. Queer in his haid. Got hurt a spell back—got shot some way. Says all kinds of anti-goddlin' foolishness." She blushed at memory of some of the things he *had* said. "He's allus talkin' funny."

"Wasn't nothin' funny," said the marshal drily, "about the way he flattened Haigler's oilers."

"Haigler!" She said it bitterly with down-curled lips. "That's the buzzard you ort t' put in jail! Polecat hired Fiori to run off with me—Fiori *said* so!"

A change disturbed the set of Durango's features. The mark of some hidden thinking put its reflection across his cheeks, turning them dour and moody, chiseling the lines in them more deeply. There were, of an instant, odd lights in his eyes, and, very gently, his left hand brushed the edge of a gun butt. He stood that way, with feet set well apart and with his pockmarked face wholly shadowed by his thoughts.

He said again, and said it doggedly: "Mebbe you better come down an' look this fellow over." And the hand that had touched his gun showed a sudden edge of whiteness as he jammed it in his pocket.

Clementine shrugged. "Where-at you holdin' him?"

"Jail's down yonder." Durango climbed into his saddle, looking faintly surprised as he saw the girl take a pair of burros from a waiting Cousin Jack and thrust a slim, tan leg across the back of the nearest. "Didn't know your ol' man owned any burros."

"He don't. These yere are Rush Rago's."

"Don't recollect ever seein' you in town

196

before. Lubbock send you in fer somethin'?"

Clementine's eyes went stormy, showing him a real and defiant anger. But she didn't answer and, after a moment, with a shrug he led off down the canyon, heading for the road that passed the Pines. They reached it and Durango's horse swung right, Clementine urging her burros after him.

Still silent, they turned up the drive to the jail yard. Ancient oaks and a pollen-laden juniper swayed their foliage in a lazy wind, and the sun, down-slanting through it, laid bright, swift moving patterns across the gopher-burrowed sand.

They swung down before the squat gray building, Clementine knotting the burros' ropes about the hitchrack.

"You goin' to cut loose of this fella if I say he's Rago?"

The marshal scrubbed his chin. "Depends," he grunted, looking hard at her. "Strikes me you're a heap interested in this jasper."

She stared down into her hands, then quickly up at him. She said defiantly: "I been figgerin' to stay in town fer a spell—keep house fer him. Don't look like I'd get much chance to do that while you got him hawg-tied in this place."

"Accordin' to your tell of it, I got no business turnin' him loose. You claim Fiori said he was takin' you to Haigler. This guy Rago—if he *is*

Rago—come bustin' into town an' tied straight off into Haigler. Don't see how I can overlook his pluggin' of them two Mexicans. Greasers wants to keep on livin' just like anybody else. Accordin' to the law—"

She said scornfully: "Who gives a damn about the law? Did the fella that killed that Y Bencher worry about it? Did Paw when he shot Fiori? Did that Lincoln County crowd? The law is what folks make it an'—"

"Not where I'm packin' the star," Durango said, and pushed open the door.

Clementine scoffed. "What about that lynch crowd workin' a sweat up?"

"That sounds," Durango growled, "like some of Haigler's doin'. I'll tend to him, an' you won't need swear out no warrant for it neither." He said it with a tightening of his pockmarked cheeks and pointed across the room. "That door right over there. Third cell to your right."

Clementine, following Durango's terse directions, found the light not so good in there. Night's gloom was already settling in the corridor. But she could see through the third cell's grating the man on the bunk with his face turned toward the wall.

She looked again. With a deep breath she cried suddenly: "That fella ain't Rush Rago!"

Durango had his look. With narrowed lids and a soft oath falling from his lips, he pulled out a bunch of keys and the lock clicked back. He was at the bunk in two quick strides, jerking the fellow over. It was Bransen. There was drying blood in his matted hair. His wrists were cased in handcuffs.

Chapter 21

ON THE LAM

Rush Rago, locked in the Tyrone jail, did a lot of thinking; most of it bitter. He sure was in a jackpot and, so far as he could see, through no especial fault of his own. It looked, he told himself resentfully, as if he were being goat for someone.

He backtracked his recent movements, trying to see if somewhere along the line there lurked an explanation—trying to see if any place he'd had the choice of doing things differently.

He'd been reading sign on Clementine's abductor when Paw had jumped him. Under Paw's gunsights he had led Paw to Lost Valley; had been run off by Paw at gun-point after Paw's killing of the conniving Buck Fiori. Arrived in Tyrone town, he had gone to the Broken Bucket to quench his thirst and rest up a bit before tackling the Company for a job. At the Broken Bucket he'd been jumped by Haigler and his two gun-wielding Mexes. In self-defense he'd put Haigler's help out of the running and been preparing to do the same by Haigler when that ugly toad of a marshal had jumped into things, coppering all the best. His present incarceration resulted from these things.

He could not see where he could have done differently—unless he'd let somebody kill him. Nor could he see any explanation . . . Well, yes; there was explanation, all right, for Paw's running him off. Like a damn fool, he'd let Paw see he knew about his mine. That had put the polish to Paw's antagonism—the wonder was Paw hadn't up and dropped him as he had Fiori.

But Haigler . . .

Wait! He'd never met Haigler in his life— hadn't known the man from Adam. Yet Haigler had known *him*. There was a significance in that fact that Rush felt a need to understand. And then he guessed it. Haigler must have been a witness to that little fracas in Lost Valley! Haigler must have been waiting there for Fiori and the girl and seen the whole damn play without tipping his hand.

But why had he jumped Rush? Rush hadn't seen him—no one had. Was he jealous of Rush's acquaintance with the girl? That didn't seem to make much sense. Maybe . . . Oho! Haigler knew Rush had heard Fiori's crack about taking the girl to Haigler; he was out to shut Rush's mouth.

In that case he'd be trying the same on Paw!

Rush wondered if Haigler was hep to Paw's mine. It sure looked mighty like it. Had Haigler been out to compromise the girl? To force her into marrying him?

It was a pretty low-down thought. Rush didn't like it, but what other explanation was there? One thing was sure: this country had a pronto way with kidnappers. If Haigler had seen a danger in Rush's knowledge of his intentions, he must see an even greater one in Paw's. It was dollars to doughnuts Haigler was on his way to Maverick Canyon right this dad-burned minute!

It made Rush feel kind of restless, thinking that way. It seemed as if he ought to be on his way out there himself. Paw was a tough old rooster, but that Haigler egg . . . And then, of course, there was the girl . . . He might not feel like marrying her— he wasn't the marrying kind—but after all he sort of owed her a bit for the way she'd nursed him through that wound—for the way she'd taken him in when he was down and out. Fact was, if it hadn't been for her, he thought, he'd probably have kicked the bucket.

A sudden thought drew in his cheeks, empha- sized muscles that cast grim shadows along his stubborn jaw. Haigler had made his play to grab the girl through Buck Fiori. Since that scheme had been a fiasco, might the man not attempt now to drop two birds with one bullet—the slug with which he'd be aiming to send Paw over the Divide? With Paw dead, he'd have the girl where he wanted her.

Rago's shoulders moved impatiently. If only he could get out of this damn jail! He'd have

Haigler hollering calf-rope or know the reason why in damn short order.

The more he thought about Haigler and the sinister aspect of Clementine's being left at the fellow's mercy, the more Rush wanted to get out. It made him feel like kicking the place down. And he *did* kick the outside wall a couple of times. It didn't make any noticeable impression though. This was a first-rate jailhouse and nobody was going to whittle himself out with any jack-knife.

He gave a closer attention to his prison. Judging by the thickness of the window-ledge, these walls were plenty thick. The window itself was out, too. It would take a regular bandsaw to cut through *those* iron bars. And the same kind of iron, hammered flat, was used in the manufacture of the cells. That left the door. And he didn't see any gilt-edged hopes pinned on that possibility, either. The door's lock was the latest thing of its kind and plenty stout. The only chance of getting out would have to lie with the jailor. Rush hadn't seen the fellow yet, unless it were that leather-faced tobacco-chewer who'd waved at him from the jail-front when he'd gone past down the road; the fellow who'd looked after him and had told the marshal "Same guy," when Durango had brought him in. Now if his keeper were this fellow, any kind of mealtime fracas might as well be chucked in the discard before given trial.

Leather-Face had the look of an hombre who had been around.

Rush sat down on his bunk and thought things over. "Where there's a will there's a way," he muttered; "or so I been led to believe. Wonder what kinda ducks think up all them clever sayin's? Bet the one that figured that out never took no meals in here."

He walked around a spell to see if that would shake his thoughts up. He'd heard more tales of fellas busting jail; some of the weirdest things, according to *their* stories, had served to get them loose. One fellow had set the jug on fire, forcing the jailor to take him out. That sounded pretty good, but if the fellow's keeper had been Leather-Face, Rush probably wouldn't have heard the story.

He'd heard of lass-ropes being hitched through the bars of a window, their other ends tied fast to freighters, so that when the wagons rolled off the window went the same direction. That had a good sound, too; but Rush, with a scowl at *his* window, decided the stunt would work best in a book.

He recalled the way young Bill Bonney had cut loose of the Lincoln courthouse. That had been a slick stunt, too; but Leather-Face might not be so handy to catch his bullet as Bob Ollinger had been. And then, this layout wasn't the same.

Oh, there were a hundred and fifty ways for

getting out of a hoosgow—but the trouble was each one of them depended on special requirements, none of which were on tap at this Tyrone lock-up.

It looked powerfully as if Rush Rago were fixed to stand trial.

And then, of a sudden, he had it—saw how he might get out. It was considerably risky and depended for its success on the quickness of Leather-Face's reactions, plus a number of other factors. But mostly it was up to Leather-Face. On how shrewd and cagey the fellow was, on how vast an indignation he could manage, on the shocking power of Rago's ruse and how quickly his keeper could get into action when the occasion demanded speed. The trick depended also, though to a lesser extent, on the pride the guy took in his office. No merciful sentiments or charitable feelings could be looked for back of Leather-Face's cud-bulged countenance; he wouldn't recognize sympathy's markings if it smacked him in the eye. But he might be proud of his record, and on that chance Rush prepared to gamble.

The first thing he did was to ease down on his bunk and carefully make himself comfortable to think out the details better. Ten minutes later he was crawling round the floor on all fours, reaching the palms of his hands into all the dusty corners he could locate, wiping the floor with them under his bunk. They would, he thought, grinning when he got to his feet, have done considerable credit to a coal-heaver. He spit on them a little, then wiped them on his face. There wasn't any mirror he could look in for the result, but with the roughness of his whiskers he guessed he looked a sight. He walked over to the cell door then and bellered for the jailor.

After a while scuffling bootsteps announced the man's approach. He was taking his time about it.

It was the leather-faced tobacco-chewer, all right. The man said crustily: "What the hell you makin' all this racket fer?"

He scowled at Rush as if he were thinking of batting Rush's ears down. Rush said placatingly: "Sorry, pardner. I don't want to be no nuisance, but I see these cells all got runnin' water an' I figured mebbe if you could find me a mirror an' a razor I'd like to clean up a little—"

"What fer? You ain't goin' no place. Think mebbe the president of the Company'll be comin' down to interview you? Or mebbe some of them West Coast reporters?"

Ignoring the fellow's scowl, Rush chuckled as if the man had made a first-class joke. "Never can tell. Stranger things've happened. Hate to go round lookin' like a dash-burned range tramp. I got a coupla dollars in my boot that's yours if you can find me them tools." Rush slipped off the boot and exhibited the two bank notes. "How about it?"

Leather-Face said dubiously: "I dunno. Boss mightn't like it. He give me strict orders—"

"O.K.," said Rush, picking up his boot and pretending that he was going to replace his money. "At least you got no objections to gettin' me a hunk of soap, have you?"

"Lemme look at them bills."

Rush passed them over.

"All right," growled Leather-Face. "I'll see what I can dig up." And, tucking Rush's money in his pocket, he shuffled off down the corridor.

He came back a few minutes later with a cloudy piece of mirror and a safety razor. "This here shaver belongs to the boss, so be dang careful how you use 'er, an' clean 'er up when you're finished." Leather-Face grunted, and pushed the articles in beneath the door.

"How about a little light?"

"Mebbe you'd like to have a brass band along with it so you can shave to ragtime?" Leather-Face snorted. "You sure want a lot of waitin' on."

"For two dollars you hadn't oughta mind throwin' in a little light."

"I'll give you ten minutes. 'F you ain't done by then it's your hard luck. I don't wanta lose my job." Leather-Face tramped off and, a moment later, a light clicked on on the ceiling.

Rush propped up the bit of mirror above the

lavatory and, making sure the razor blade was screwed in tight, proceeded to shave himself in a hurry. Turning on the tap, he got as much of the dirt off the rest of his face as possible. Then, unscrewing the razor, he lifted out its blade, cleaned it and, praying there weren't too many germs left on it by previous users, drew it lightly across his left wrist, being very careful not to sever anything more dangerous to continued health than skin.

Blood flowed. He made a second light incision. More blood flowed. Dropping the razor blade on the floor, he squeezed the cuts. By the time his allotted ten minutes was up he had a bloody enough wrist to give a pretty fair imitation of suicide—at a distance. Then, artfully disposing himself in a crumpled heap along the floor, and with his bloody wrist turned toward the corridor, he fixed his eyes in a glassy stare and waited.

Leather-Face didn't give him above three minutes more than he'd promised. Scuffling boots in the corridor announced his return. With a prayer for luck, Rush cocked his muscles.

Leather-Face took one look and swore. Still swearing, he got out his keys and in a fine sweat jerked open the door and sprang across the threshold. With alarm and anger flaring across his face, he dropped to a crouch above Rago, reaching for the bleeding wrist.

He was like that, off balance, reaching,

when Rago grabbed him. One strong brown hand clamped a vice-like hold on Bransen's outstretched arm; a booted foot drove sledge-like against Bransen's nearest shin. Bransen went down with an enraged howl, and Rush bounded over on top of him.

A big man, Bransen, but soft and flabby from too great attention to politics. Rush had the man's own handcuffs locked about Bransen's wrists before the jailor got his breath back. With grinning jocularity Rush whipped off the fellow's neckerchief and stuffed it in his spluttering mouth, reducing Bransen's threats to unintelligible gurgles.

Rush stepped back to survey his work. "C'mon, baboon. Up on your feet!" He helped him up with a hand gripped in his collar, his left hand deftly sliding Bransen's gun from its open-topped holster. "Get over on that bunk an' don't waste any time."

Bransen glowered. But when Rush raised the pistol's barrel suggestively, the jailor's belligerence wilted. He waddled over to the bunk. "Lay down an' face the wall," Rush ordered, and when the man had done so, whipped off the fellow's belt and securely lashed his ankles.

"Happy dreams," Rush said, and tapped Bransen on the head to make sure the fellow behaved himself. Then he pulled the blanket up over Bransen's bulk and, stepping out into the corridor, clanged the cell door shut.

"That you, Rag?"

That whispered call stopped Rush like a bullet. Keys in one hand, Bransen's gun in the other, he'd been fixing to find the way out. He stood rigid now, bent forward, listening, with his eyes two frosty slits.

Rago! It was the second time today that name had been used in connection with him. When Haigler'd named his Rago it had struck no chord in his memory; but it struck one now. He remembered who he was with a bang. He wheeled his torso round. "Where are you?"

"Over here. Two cells back."

Rush catfooted over in a hurry. The reflection from his own lit cell showed a whiskered visage pressed against the grill.

"Stevens!"

"Yeah," said the desert rat drily. "Imagine meetin' you here. Got the key to this dang door?"

"Got any more gold rush yarns?"

"Aw—you don't hold that ag'in' me, do you?" Stevens wheedled. "I'm in a awful jackpot. That dang Durango's goin' to hev my scalp if I don't cut loose of here."

"I'll listen, if you make it quick," Rush said. "But you better tell the truth this time—an' never mind the varnish. What'd you hand me that story for?"

"It was Durango's play. I'm givin' it to you Gospel. I used to work fer Lubbock, an' Durango had found out about his mine. When Lubbock fired me fer gettin' likkered up an' talkin', I come into town here pretty mad. Durango said if I'd go 'way off some place an' hook somebody into comin' over here on a gold hunt, he'd split Lubbock's mine with me. Like a dang ol' fool, I swallered it."

"Don't make sense to me," Rush grunted. "What'd he want to rope in a stranger for?"

"I dunno. But I'll tell you what I think. I figger he was aimin' to bump the ol' man off an' wanted some stranger handy for a goat. Reckon—"

"Reckon I'll leave you in here," Rush said coldly. "Do you good to meditate on your sins—"

"God! Don't do that, pard!" Stevens' voice shook. "Durango's changed his mind. He's goin' to bump ol' Lubbock down his shaft hole an' claim I done it! You wouldn't leave a ol' man like me to face—"

"By cripes," Rush said, "I ought to. Serve you right, you ornery ol' vinegaroon." He thought a minute. "I'll break you out if you'll give me your oath—"

"I'll give you anything—"

"Uh-uh. You're too damn eager. Reckon I better leave you right where you are. You're too durn unreliable to be floatin' round this country loose."

Rush wasted no more time. Ignoring the old bamboozler's threats and cursing, he let himself out of Justice Court and, sticking to the deepest shadows, headed uptown by a tree-darkened trail that paralleled the road.

Chapter 22

CLEAR THE TRAIL!

Rush felt pretty thankful the Tyrone jail was back such a piece from the road, because it still was light, and even in the shadow of the trees, if anyone happened to see him there'd be fireworks sure as Christmas. A horse was what he wanted, and he wasn't in a mood to care whose horse it was, either, just so it was good and fast. It was high time he was lamming it for Maverick Canyon if he aimed to square his debt and save Paw's neck for the girl. That Haigler wasn't the sort to let any grass grow under his feet; and, figuring he'd neatly put Rush's windpipe in a rope, he'd be in something of a lather to do the same by Paw. Of course Rush recalled now it was Clementine who'd shot him, but she'd given plenty of warning and had nursed him onto his feet again, and, anyway, a debt was a debt and long as Paw was her old man it was up to Rush to do his best. Most generally, he reflected, calico was calico, but Clementine's measure had been torn from a brand-new bolt; it had unusual merit. Fact was, he was getting round to the point where he'd just as soon get hooked up with her as not. Life with Clementine was hardly likely to get monotonous.

He stopped abruptly, a tag-end of movement in the yonder road halting him with blue eyes narrowed in amazement. There were two riders on that road; a guy with a star on his vest and a girl in patched man's clothing astride one burro and leading another. The man was Les Durango, the marshal—no mistaking that saturnine, pock-marked visage. But it was the girl that cocked Rush's muscles, pulled the breath clean out of his gullet. Poor light, distance and all else not-withstanding, he had recognized her instantly. It was Clementine; and the sight of her in Durango's company dragged from Rush a bitter curse.

He did not have any need to wonder why she rode with the marshal; no one rode with him from choice. Some way, for some reptilian if obscure purpose, Durango had arrested her—was taking her to jail.

For a moment Rush saw red. All his willpower, all his stamina was required to throttle the terrible impulse that came over him to drive a bullet through the fellow, to smash him crumpling from his horse. Every fiber of Rush's body, every instinct, urged him to kill the man without compunction. Star or no star, yonder rode the one-time tool of Texas politicians—the man who'd dropped a Black Range rancher for a satchelful of silver. It looked bleak indeed for Clementine to be found traveling in his company.

But good horse sense and a saving need for

knowledge finally pulled Rush's gun down. The roaring blood receded from his head, his sight grew clear and he got the cramp out of his muscles. He would dog their tracks and find out what was up. If foxy Les tried to hold that girl in his jail, his sins and contrivings were due to catch up with him in mighty short order.

To think with Rush was to act. He saw things stripped to their bare essentials, and few mental quirks had ever been known to sway him from a purpose. As Rago saw it, right or wrong had not the slightest part in this grim business. The basic facts were these: Clementine was a free agent, bound by nothing but her relationship to Paw. If Durango in his guise of marshal attempted in any way interference with that status—tried to clip her wings or any other damn skulduggery—he was due to get clipped himself!

He arrived at the jail not thirty steps behind them; heard Clementine say to Durango: "You goin' to cut loose of that fella if I say he's Rago?" and heard the marshal's enigmatic reply. He heard, too, Durango's remarks concerning himself, Fiori, Haigler and his two Mex friends. And then the girl and the star-packer had swung from their saddles and he was watching them stride inside.

Soft-stepping as a cat, Rush went in right after the marshal. He followed them far as the door to the cell corridor, grinning bleakly as he heard

215

their exclamations when the hogtied Bransen was discovered. Then Stevens' voice piped up and he decided to take a hand.

He had snapped the cell light off on his way out, a thoughtful gesture that now stood him in good stead. With steps no louder than a spider's, and with Bransen's gun held ready, he slipped down the murky corridor till he came outside his erstwhile abode where the muttering Durango fumbled with the knots that bound the neckerchief in Leather-Face's mouth.

Just as he was making ready to announce himself, the girl, whose back, like the others', was toward him, asked Durango: "This the lobo claimed his name was Ed Cotton?"

What Durango said wasn't fit to print; and for good measure he added, his attention still taken up by Rush's recalcitrant knots: "Stay right where you are! Don't stir a step till I get through with this. Your precious Rago's pulled a jail-break, an' you're goin' to damn well stay right here till I get my hands on him! I'm goin' to show—"

"You're goin' to shout, too, ain't you?" Rush said grimly, and shoved his gun in the marshal's back.

Durango whirled like a cat swapping ends, but Rush was ready for him. He brought the barrel of Bransen's pistol crashing down across the marshal's forehead, and Durango went down like a pole-axed steer. Not a sound and not a movement.

Rush stooped, got the marshal's keys and grunted: "Let's go." He pushed Clementine ahead of him into the shadowed corridor. "Oh, Rush—" she began, but Rush broke in with an urgent curtness.

"Not time for talk now. We got to ride—an' what I mean is *ride!*"

"Ride where?" They had reached the entrance; Durango's horse and the burros were ahead of them.

"Maverick Canyon—"

"But I don't want to go back there, Rush. I've come to keep house for you or—"

Rush gave her a quick hard look. "That's right down fine of you," he said. "But I got no house to keep an' it wouldn't be fittin' if I had one. I'll be no help to runaway girls. You're goin' back to Maverick—"

"I won't!" She drew herself up erect. "I'll not go a step!"

"Oh, yes you will," he grunted, and before she could lift a hand he grabbed her up bodily and slapped her down in Durango's saddle. In a twinkling he was up behind her, and the outraged bronc, after a few half-hearted jumps, kicked up his heels and bolted in the direction Rago guided him.

Chapter 23

RUSH MAKES UP HIS MIND

Always the exponent of grace and urbanity, of suave effrontery, of cool, quick-witted roguery, Joe Karvel, master of the just-so phrase and gesture, stepped out of character and cursed.

Bitterly and sharply he cursed the man before him; cursed him with an edge of strain tramping through the savagery of his epithets. But the figure in the old Prince Albert never moved. Like a thing hacked out of sandstone, like a bastion of the mountain, he remained where he was, unblinking, unyielding; the eyes beneath those bushy brows immutable and fixed.

That stare was like a judgment.

With silent vehemence Karvel cursed the folly that had brought him up this trail, cursed old Lubbock for refusing him an entrance, cursed his black-masked hombre for refusing to let him by.

His nerve was cracking. It could not much longer stand the obscure threat, the uncertainty of this man's unguessable intentions. That baleful, never-swerving stare had sapped his muscles of response. He had his gun in hand, but command of this situation had long ago passed from him. The will to fire was in him strongly—an urgent, clamorous thing; but there was paralysis in his finger. He could not squeeze the trigger.

For ten long minutes they had stood like this— Karvel raging, steadily growing more desperate, a toad chained by a snake's stare; the masked man saying nothing, doing nothing—a statue breaking Karvel's will.

Joe Karvel cried abruptly, hoarsely, frantically: "For God's sake get it over! Don't stand there starin' like a ninny! Say something—do something or get out of the way!"

He might as well not have spoken for all the change it evoked. The masked man neither moved nor answered. It was uncanny. It was maddening.

Karvel said: "If it's Lubbock you've come here after, don't wait around on me. I've no interest in your business here at all! All I want is to get out of here. I—" He clutched at a sudden thought. "If it's my help you want, you've only to say the word."

And still the masked man stood there—silent, unyielding, grimly patient as the stars.

It dragged a final curse from the man who straw-bossed the Y Bench. Karvel's command of himself was gone. The last vestige of his poise was shattered utterly, crumpled and consumed by his own imagination. He was a shaking, shivering, jibbering wreck.

And now at last the masked man spoke. He said

dispassionately: "You're just like Forney. I guess you're needin' Forney's medicine."

Ignoring Karvel's pistol, he produced his own. Unhurriedly he drew it from a pocket of his coat, and when the echoes had dimmed away he stood alone upon the trail.

Another man, desiring converse with old Lubbock, would have pounded on the door or shouted through it. Most men, wanting to get at Lubbock, would have battered down the door, or tried to, or would have cudgelled their brains to find some ruse—as Karvel had—to induce Paw to open it. But this was not the masked man's way. He did, as he had done with Karvel—nothing. Eighteen years of waiting had taught him something. It had stood him in good stead with Forney; with Joe Karvel. By Lubbock's door he lounged against the sandstone cliff. To a man who'd waited eighteen years, another hour or two meant little. If daylight caught him out of Tyrone town, there were always other places; he didn't *have* to go back there—Tyrone held nothing for him if success crowned his efforts here. He took the neckerchief from his face, folded his arms and lounged against the cliff. Curiosity would bring Paw out . . . It was just a matter of time.

Horse sound, drifting along with the breeze, came to him after a while; drew down his bushy brows and deepened somewhat the furrows that ran from his lips to his nostrils. That sound sent a hand halfway to the pocket where he'd put the neckerchief that had kept his identity from Karvel. But then he shrugged, refolding the arm across the other. There were just two others in this game: Haigler and Durango. Yon hurrying horse would be packing one of those—what difference which? It would be interesting to see the fellow's face when recognition came.

He made no move to secure his gun. Trust in his ability was faith; it had been a bulwark for eighteen years. That ability would serve him now.

Where he lounged against the cliff he stood in shadow, but the man dismounting from the horse below was plainly limned in the moon's bright light. The man was Haigler. Sardonic humor quirked the watcher's lips as Haigler started up the trail. That humor still was on them when Haigler, with a startled oath, stopped short three steps away.

Haigler's hand dropped hipward nervously. "That—that you, Lubbock?"

He could see the odd way Haigler canted forward, peering worriedly, striving to make out who stood in the cave's deep shadows.

But he said nothing.

As with Karvel, his silence got on Haigler's nerves. Whipping out his gun, Haigler came a short step forward; scowling, came another. The gun abruptly wavered. "Well for cripes' sake, Ruddabaugh! What are you doin' here?" And then his voice broke off in a frantic curse. He must have realized all at once the danger Ruddabaugh's presence there implied. Ruddabaugh was a wheel chair man—a man who could not walk. The muzzle of his gun jerked up, belched flame.

Too late.

Haigler was falling when he fired.

A long while later the door of Lubbock's cave-house opened; slowly, carefully, inch by cautious inch. A rifle's barrel caught the gleam of refracted moonlight. A dragging pause marked its appearance. Then Lubbock's lank shape showed vaguely in the opening; came through it and crouched, stoop-shouldered, above the two still forms sprawled prostrate in the cave's moon-silvered entrance.

He stood crouched like some old buzzard above his prey, and suddenly chuckled. Leaning his rifle against the wall, he stooped, stretching out a hand to the nearest of the silent shapes.

"Find it easier, do you, robbing dead men, Gable?"

Those insolently drawled words froze Lubbock in his tracks. It were as though Death's own hand had fallen on his shoulder, he stood that still. The wrinkled, sunken cheeks took on the shade of untouched parchment. He crouched there, stiff, unmoving—without breathing, almost.

"You remember me, don't you, Gable?" the soft voice prompted.

Dazed, without turning, almost without awareness, the man who was known to the Tyrone country as Paw Lubbock nodded.

Inexorably, the voice rolled on—as unchecked as some mighty river; as menacing as the drum of Doom. Soft it was and slyly chuckling, the tone of a man hard-steeped in satisfaction. The cadences were those of one to whom a vengeance eighteen years delayed was just as sweet as though the wrong had been dealt him yesterday.

"Remember the Belle of Joplin, Gable? You remember Lysla, don't you? How you and she put in your time together while her husband—that damn apostate Mormon—went out in the fields he hated and with the sweat of his aching body harvested crops for the money that kept her in luxury? You remember her, don't you, Gable?"

With a shudder Lubbock bowed his head. "Yes," he said in a voice scarcely above a whisper. "I've remembered her, Challoner—God knows how I've remembered her . . ."

Ruddabaugh's lips spread in a mirthless grin. "And the Mormon, Gable? You remember him? Turn around and take a look at me."

In the grip of something greater than his own reluctant will, Paw Lubbock turned. It was the creaking, buckling movement of a man whose

223

race is run. He staggered—would have collapsed entirely but for the hand he thrust to the wall—when his lifting glance collided with the man stepping out of the shadows. He shrank back, dragging a shaking hand across incredulous eyes—kept that hand before him as though to ward off a certain blow. He was mumbling; it was like the whimpering of a frightened cur.

Ruddabaugh's smile did lip service. "So you thought me dead and buried, eh? I'm not the man to be killed with quite that ease, my friend. Friend—that has a mellow sound. We *were* friends, weren't we, Gable?" He left off his baiting, his voice going abruptly bleak. "Are you ready for atonement?"

Paw shivered, and his wild, bright eyes showed a wholly animal pleading. "Challoner—Challoner . . ." His voice went husky; broke. "God knows how I've repented—"

"Repented? Hah! I've done that myself. It's not enough. What is it the Scriptures tell us? An eye for an eye? An eye's not much, is it, Gable? They tell me you've discovered gold . . . ?"

"Yes—yes!" Lubbock jumped at it eagerly. "A wonderful mine, Challoner—wonderful. Gold, yes; and almost pure—a whole great wall of it, Challoner. I've barely scratched the surface—"

"Take me there. I'll look at it."

But Ruddabaugh's voice held no promise. Nor did he tell Paw that he knew Clementine was in town—that he'd seen her there and that while she was in the restaurant he'd extracted something from the pack she had not removed from Rush's second burro. Or that that something was in his pocket; or that even now he was casting about in his mind, hunting a scheme for the thing's best employment.

Paw led him through the door in the cave-house shack's back wall and into the tunnel where Rush had found the bulging gunnysacks. He did not pause but strode ahead with rapid strides, his chagrin and fear at the fate that had overtaken him fading in the hope for continued life. Deeper and deeper they went, piercing the mountain's very vitals, the flickering candle throwing their moving shadows grotesquely against the timbered walls; and with the sound of purling water growing ever louder in their ears till it became a thunderous roar, preventing talk entirely, drowning even the sound of their footfalls.

Rounding a bend in the tunnel's passage, they came at last in sight of a waterfall. A mighty avalanche of waters poured from some place in the unseen dark above, cascading down with the rush of a mill-race to become an underground river that went gurgling off into other darkness through the mist of spray that lashed their faces.

Paw stopped with Ruddabaugh's hand on his

shoulder. With lips squeezed against Paw's ear, the man in the Prince Albert shouted: "Where in hell is the mine?"

And well might he ask, for the waterfall stopped all progress.

But Lubbock grinned. He took Ruddabaugh's arm and pointed. Straight at the falling waters he waved that outstretched hand. "Back there!" He made no sound, but Ruddabaugh read his lips.

"Behind that water?" He was eyeing it, scowling, when Paw nodded.

Paw set off, the candle spluttering, making strange patterns in the mist. Ruddabaugh trod on his heels, a naked pistol gripped in his fist, alert for the slightest trickery.

But Paw's mind at this juncture had no room for guile. Clear around to the right he led, and suddenly, with leaping heart, Ruddabaugh saw the tiny ledge that led behind the pounding waters. Shielding his candle, Paw stepped out. Ruddabaugh followed with care.

They were in another cavern, the lashing of the waters muffled by a turn of the sandstone wall. Paw was pointing; and, looking, Ruddabaugh saw by the flickering candlelight a hanging ledge of dull, soft-gleaming metal. If ever there had been a mother lode, then this was it.

The eyes looking out from beneath his tangled brows showed a fleeting humor. "Yes," he murmured consideringly, "it's a great find, Gable. Be something for you to think about when you've tired of reflecting on the pass that brought you to—this end." He stared at the old man reflectively, a faint half-smile tugging queerly at his lips.

"What—what do you mean?" Paw's gaunt, stooped shoulders stiffened.

Ruddabaugh brought a little bundle from his pocket, undid it and held its contents out for Paw to see. "Guess you know what this stuff is? . . . Yes, it's dynamite. And here's the cap and here's the fuse. Take a good long look at them, Gable; they're goin' to settle the score you've had outstanding all these years."

Paw stared at the objects, fascinated. He looked at the faint half-smile still curling Ruddabaugh's mouth, and an ague seemed to seize him. He thrust his shaking hands behind him, backing till his shoulders rubbed against the precious wall.

"You can't do it, Challoner!" He cried: "You'll not—you'll never dare! That wall is worth a fortune!"

Ruddabaugh laughed, a low and gloating laugh that drove the last of the faded color from Paw's cheeks. He said: "Have no fear, old friend. I'm not destroying your pretty mine—nor taking it from you, either. It'll be here when the Trumpet blows. I'm leaving you here to guard it." He looked at Paw and laughed again. "Mebbe Lysla's ghost will come and keep you company."

"You're—you're killing me, then?"

"Not I. Hunger'll do that for me—or madness. Madness or hunger, one or the other."

"In God's name," Lubbock cried, "what is it you've got in mind?"

"Wait," Ruddabaugh said, and with a smile wheeled round the bend. Paw, when he came back, was where he'd left him.

"What is it? I'll tell you. There's nothing complex about it. I had other plans, but this is better. I'm going to seal you in this cavern alive; I'm going to leave you with your gold and with your thoughts to wait for hunger. Don't waste time hoping for escape. With all that dynamite, I'll bring half the mountain down on that tunnel. Men's acts catch up with them, Gable; you robbed me, but you'll not rob God."

With a malignant smile, pistol held at his hip and ready, Ruddabaugh backed to the bend. "The shots are placed, the fuses hissing. I'll have to go now. Pleasant thoughts, my friend, and au revoir."

Ruddabaugh's departure was cut short by his reappearance. "I'm afraid I'll have to have that candle, Ed. *Stay where you are.* I'll get it."

And he did.

The sound of his hurrying boots receded from the darkness of the cavern that held Paw Lubbock and his mine. They echoed briefly from the passage leading to the waterfall; were cut abruptly short by a startled cry—by the slithering sound of a body falling. The candle's faint glow vanished. An anguished moan crept softly through the blackness, terrible with its cargo of dread realization. "Gable! Gable, it's my leg . . . I think I've broke it. Quick, man—*hurry!*"

But Paw Lubbock stayed where he was. And, suddenly, a mighty flash lit the place like day; and on its heels a roar to split the eardrums made the mountain lurch and shiver. It was followed by the grinding slide of rock. . . .

They were almost at the place where the trail turned into the canyon when Rush and the girl felt the ground shake wildly beneath the plunging feet of their frightened horse. It took all Rush's strength to fight the animal down; to quiet it in the muffled, booming roar that followed.

"Dynamite!" Rush said, and whistled softly. And the girl half turned in the saddle to explore his moonlit face with questioning eyes.

But "Shh!" Rush muttered, and sat listening with canted head while the horse stamped restlessly, plainly anxious to be gone. "By George, Clem—Listen! D'you hear it?"

She said with a puzzled stare. "That's water, ain't it?"

"It sure is. Didn't you tell me there was a waterfall back in that cavern? That underground river you said old Proctor was so anxious to get hold of, ain't it? Well, somethin' tells me he's goin' to get his wish! That's water, all right, an' it's comin' like the devil beatin' tanbark! Any way out of this place?"

"Ahead just a bit there's a trail that leads up to the rim—"

"Hold tight! I'm goin' to try for it," Rush said gruffly, and put his spurs to work with a will.

The horse leaped forward. Tired as it was, it responded to Rush's steel-tipped demands. It wanted to get out of that place, too, and stretched its legs to a racking gallop.

Ahead, like a tide of shimmering silver, the crest of the plunging waters shoved its head above the canyon floor. It was like a sparkling wall in the moon's blue glare; a wall that rolled and tossed and roared as it rushed toward them like an avalanche.

The horse didn't like that view at all. Fatigue forgotten, he wanted to turn and bolt. It took all Rush's will, all his brawn and curses to keep the cayuse facing it. And then Clementine, her tones hollow with her own fright, cried: "Quick! Turn right! That trail—"

Rush swung the horse's head, and they went clattering up the slope. Up and up and up, till finally the pitch gave way to rolling yucca-studded grasslands, and they slid from the pony's back and trotted over to the rim, with Rush holding grimly fast to the snorting animal's reins.

It looked as if they'd gotten out just in time. The canyon floor was lost beneath the swirl of churning waters. Rush felt the girl's hand tighten on his arm. Following her gaze, he started, cursed. Water surged from the cave-house entrance as though from a mighty hydrant; it was shooting a good twenty feet straight outward from the cliff-face to fall, a glittering cascade of molten silver, to the canyon rocks below.

He held her while she sobbed, face hard-pressed against his chest. The same thought occupied the mind of each: If Paw had been in that cave . . .

But there was nothing they could do. Rush told her so. "Someone's blasted that river loose, an' all hell can't stop it now. Paw's done, if he was in there." He clenched his jaw, savagely glaring at the roaring waters; comforting the girl as best he could.

And after a while—

"Might's well head back for town, I reckon," he told her gently. "Be hours before that stream goes down—if it *goes* down; which it don't look like it's goin' to."

He helped her into the saddle and climbed wearily up behind her. He was tired, yes; but not so weary he'd forgotten the thrill of holding her in his arms.

He said, much later: "About that notion you was mentionin' . . . Uh—that housekeeper's job—"

"I've done changed my mind. I don't want charity—"

"Charity! Great Scott, girl! Who's talkin' about charity?" Rush glowered, his face ferocious with its scowl. "What I got in mind's a ring. I was goin' to say I couldn't use no housekeeper. But I'm lookin' fer a wife. Er . . . reckon you could fill the bill?"

The look she gave him made it plain she could and would.

Center Point Large Print
600 Brooks Road / PO Box 1
Thorndike, ME 04986-0001 USA

(207) 568-3717

US & Canada:
1 800 929-9108
www.centerpointlargeprint.com